Werewolf
On
Madison Avenue

Published in the United States of America
ISBN   Paperback: 978-1-959761-43-3
ISBN   Hardback: 978-1-959761-47-1
ISBN   eBook: 978-1-959761-44-0

The opinions expressed by the author are not necessarily those of ReadersMagnet, LLC.

ReadersMagnet, LLC
10620 Treena Street, Suite 230 | San Diego, California, 92131 USA
1.619. 354. 2643 | www.readersmagnet.com

Book design copyright © 2022 by ReadersMagnet, LLC. All rights reserved.

Cover design by Kent Gabutin
Interior design by Ched Celiz

WEREWOLF
ON
MADISON AVENUE

BY EDWARD R. LIPINSKI

ReadersMagnet, LLC

Dedicated to my brother Joseph

CHAPTER 1

Madison Avenue, is the thoroughfare in the heart of New York City, the legendary concourse that is the capital of the advertising world, the citadel of salesmanship, the Mecca of marketing, the hub of hype, the podium of product push, the street of sizzle, the rostrum of razzle-dazzle, and the bastion of bamboozle. Every day in the many glass and steel office towers along this famous avenue, brigades of creative geniuses meet and brainstorm new ways to convince the multitude of consumers around the world that they cannot live without a plethora of products that most of them had never even heard of until the barrage of advertisements forced its way into their collective consciousness.

It is here on Madison Avenue that some of the biggest names in the business made their reputations. People like J. Walter Thompson, David Ogilvy and Bill Bernbach, built the modern world of advertising by writing creative copy and launching brilliant campaigns that made advertising entertaining as well as informative and effective. Unfortunately, not all the names associated with Madison Avenue advertising are as highly regarded as the three above.

One name that particularly sends shudders of revulsion down the spine of any respectable ad man is the name Cudmore. For it was the Cudmore brothers, Damon and Pythias, who used their raunchy imaginations to sink advertising to the lowest depths of tastelessness by creating a style that bordered on the barbaric.

Damon and Pythias made their careers by committing the ultimate unpardonable, transgression—at least on Madison Avenue: together they became the supreme purveyors of bad taste in advertising. Their ads were so trashy that for Madison Avenue, and probably the rest of the marketing world, the name Cudmore became a synonym for raunchy, schlock marketing. Many in the Madison Avenue crowd referred to the Cudmores as the Crudmores because it seemed that was what the brothers produced—more and more crud. Another sobriquet applied to Damon and Pythias was "the crud and crap duo."

There was considerable justification for these judgments. After all, it was Damon Cudmore who came up with the slogan, "It'll come out all right in the end!" for Smooth-Ease Laxatives. And it was Pythias who coined the term, "the proper stopper" for Feminique Tampons. And one, or both of them, created the concept of "an over-the-shoulder-boulder-holder" for Lovely Lady Lilly-soft Brassieres.

Damon was one who launched the ad campaign for Formula 6 hemorrhoid cream with the maxim, "Baste your booty with Formula 6 and erase your whole pain." In print that ad didn't seem so bad, but when people heard it on the radio they came to suspect that word *whole* was actually a double-entendre with a not-so-subtle message in the subtext.

In addition to writing incredibly bad advertising, the Cudmore brothers were also unmitigated scoundrels, employing every underhanded, cutthroat means to secure new clients, eradicate competition, and plaster the media with coarse and vulgar ad campaigns. At times it seemed that there were no bounds to what their tasteless imagination or conniving ruthlessness could come up with. It was those ad campaigns and the unrelenting drive to secure, and even steal new clients that made the rest of Madison Avenue cringe and pray for their eventual demise.

When Damon and Pythias started out on Madison Avenue they founded the Cudmore & Cudmore Advertising Agency. During their early years in the business together, they seemed like the ideal crud team, two brothers who worked in harmony dreaming up ridiculously inane ad campaigns that caused ripples of revulsion up and down Madison Avenue and the consumer world. This brotherly love and mutual admiration apparently started when the Cudmore boys were born. Their parents chose the names Damon and Pythias for them, thinking that like the two comrades of ancient Greece, their sons would grow up to be the best of friends, inseparable as a harmonious and loving duo.

At first, during the early decades of their life together, that prophecy was, in fact, a reality. Throughout childhood and continuing through their school years, the two were inseparable as brothers, buddies and tried-and-true comrades. After school they entered the work force and found jobs working in advertising for the same company. Later, using money they had inherited, they decided to start their own advertising agency together, and they set up a company which they called Cudmore & Cudmore.

All went well for the first few years of their business. The two brothers, using their typical mixture of chicanery and scheming, sprinkled with generous helpings of bad taste, managed to bring in a number of high-paying accounts and promoted their clients' products with an unbelievable flair for creative vulgarity.

At that time, it seemed that together they had forged a viable, working, and amicable partnership and were on the road to establishing a successful, enduring ad agency. The fact that the rest of the advertising world held them in contempt never seemed to bother either brother and together they continued, oblivious to the scorn of the world around them.

But then something happened between them—no one knows exactly what—and they had a falling out. At that point the two siblings who were once the best of friends, now became the bitterest of enemies and fiercest of rivals. After the break-up of their partnership, both brothers tried to disguise the fact that they were related or that they even resembled each other. To that end Pythias Cudmore remained clean shaven while his brother grew a broad mustache. Damon Cudmore parted his hair while Pythias combed his mane straight back.

These changes, however, were only superficial and cosmetic. Underneath, in their hearts, minds, and souls, they remained of the same breed, two men cast from the same mold. Both were unscrupulous, conniving, arrogant, and driven, extremely self-confident with a relentless drive to get to the top at all costs.

Pythias moved out of the Cudmore & Cudmore Agency to set up his own company further south on Madison Avenue and 28th street. Damon shortened the name of his agency to The Cudmore Advertising Agency.

Pythias couldn't use the Cudmore name for his company because his rotten brother had already taken it. He thought over a number of names and at one point even considered spelling Cudmore backwards to become Eromduc. But as he thought more about it, he realized that Eromduc sounded more like a pharmaceutical product for diarrhea than a corporate appellation so he discarded that idea.

In the end he decided to call his company the Triumph Agency. He chose Triumph because it suggested victory, and that's what Pythias wanted. He was out for blood, and one day he hoped to vanquish Damon and reign supreme on Madison Avenue as the sole surviving Cudmore brother and high potentate of the advertising world.

Thus, began a rivalry and blood feud that lasted right up to the present day. With each passing year, the feud intensified in competition and rivalry. Each brother plummeted to new depths of malevolence as they employed the dastardliest tricks and underhanded subterfuges to steal the other's clients thereby hoping to put the opposing brother out of business. But since both brothers were equally matched in Machiavellian intellect and chicanery, neither could gain the upper hand. So, the struggle eventually settled into a draw with both Damon and Pythias surviving. Nevertheless, they remained hostile adversaries, ever vigilant for an advantage, ever eager to gain the upper hand. This uneasy tension crackled along Madison Avenue.

Initially, the admen from other agencies on Madison Avenue looked on this feud with anticipation, many in the advertising world praying fervently for the eventual annihilation of one or both of the brothers. They watched the rivalry from the sidelines, hoping that at some point Damon and Pythias would challenge each other in a duel to the death.

Indeed, at one time or another, it seemed that almost everyone in the advertising world dreamed and yearned for a complete Cudmore extinction. If that happened, then surely Madison Avenue would be a better, cleaner, fresher environment for all civilized, dedicated admen. But even though all of Madison Avenue prayed for the end of the two brothers, it never happened because the breakup of the Cudmore & Cudmore Agency seemed to charge each brother with renewed vigor, making each more determined than ever to succeed at any cost—plastering vulgar ads in every form of media.

And even though the battle between the two brothers was spirited vigorous and sprayed with venom, it remained confined to words, obscene gestures, mud-slinging, and unscrupulous business tactics.

Some of the more pious folk on Madison Avenue prayed that divine intervention might see fit to strike down one or both of the brothers with a heart attack or brain seizure. But for some reason, the divinity above chose to turn a deaf ear to the marketing mayhem that ran amok on Madison Avenue. The only thing that the respectable admen of Madison Avenue could do was duck for cover and pray that somehow, like the Smooth-Ease Laxatives, it would all come out right in the end.

CHAPTER 2

Sometime after the Cudmores separated to go their own ways, an energetic and optimistic young man by the name of Jefferson Raymond Foxlove applied for work in Damon Cudmore's Agency.

Jeff Foxlove was a graduate from the City College in New York with a degree in business administration. Fresh out of college, he wasn't sure exactly what he wanted to do in the business world but he'd recently read *Confessions of an Advertising Man* by David Ogilvy. The book was essentially an autobiography of Ogilvy's career on Madison Avenue. In the book, Ogilvy told how he started up his own advertising agency and built it into one of world's biggest by creating advertising that was informative, direct, effective, and above all, honest. That book inspired Jeff and charged him with the enthusiasm to become an advertising man in the Ogilvy mold.

He sent out his résumé to all the ad agencies in New York City hoping to land some sort of position with the big guns of Madison Avenue. Unfortunately, no one was hiring just then and he got no response to his many submissions. Just when he thought that the doors to the advertising world were never to open, he received a call from someone at the Cudmore Advertising Agency. It was an invitation to come to the office for an interview.

Now Jefferson Foxlove was a virtual babe in the woods when it came to the advertising community. He knew the names of some of the big agencies like Saatchi & Saatchi, and B.B.D & O, Ogilvy, Benson & Mather, and Young & Rubicam, but he had never heard of the Cudmore Agency so he knew nothing about the Cudmore rivalry or about the sleazy reputation of either brother. All Jefferson knew was that he had an interview with an advertising agency on Madison Avenue and the prospect that he might actually work as an adman fired him with anticipation and excitement.

On the appointed day for his interview, Jeff put on his best blue business suit—actually his only business suit—and went to the Cudmore Advertising Agency. He expected that he would meet with someone in the human resources department, but much to his astonishment he was told that he would meet with the supreme honcho, the great enchilada himself, the president of the agency, Mr. Damon Cudmore.

Jeff was invited into Cudmore's office and offered a seat. He sat down in a rigid chair facing a big desk, behind which sat Damon Cudmore. For a few moments neither man spoke. Cudmore sat behind his desk reading over Jeff's résumé while Jeff sat erect in his chair, his hands folded on his lap, staring in reverent silence at the man sitting behind the desk before him.

He judged Cudmore to be somewhere in his mid-fifties, tall, with a good physique, a full head of dark brown hair with touches of gray at the temples and sideburns and a broad, dark moustache. When Cudmore looked up from the résumé and over his glasses at Jeff, his eyes appeared sharp, piercing, and unblinking. For a long moment those eyes remained focused on the younger man. Jeff met that intense stare with as much concentration as he could muster and hoped that he was looking confident and self-assured, even though, internally, his stomach was doing somersaults.

Finally, after a long moment of intense scrutiny, Cudmore spoke.

"So, you're a recent graduate of City College."

"Yes sir."

"With a major in business."

"Yes sir."

"And never had any experience in advertising."

"No sir, but I'm willing to learn." Jeff tried to make that last part sound as enthusiastic as possible.

The hard features of Cudmore's face softened a little and a slight smile formed on his tight lips. He thought to himself that this is what he wanted, a young man fresh out of college with no experience and no pre-conceived notions as to what advertising was all about. He perceived in Jeff a warm body with a blank mind; fresh clay that he could mold and shape.

"Do you know anything about me or my agency? About the kind of advertising we do here?"

"No sir, I'm sorry I haven't had time to do much in the way of research, but—"

Damon Cudmore silenced him with an upraised hand. This was even better, not only was this young man an eager beaver, but he was also an innocent virgin in the advertising world, totally unaware of the notorious reputation of the Cudmore Agency.

"Don't apologize, my boy. Previous knowledge is not necessary. I'll teach you everything you need to know. Now, when can you start?"

"You mean I'm hired?"

"Yes, I think that you'll work out fine here so I'm willing to give you a trial shot. When can you come to work?"

"Well, I can come in tomorrow."

"Good, good! The sooner the better." And Cudmore meant that. He wanted to get this young Foxlove boy under his wing as soon as possible so he could insulate him from any Madison Avenue gossip that might sour him.

Cudmore was all smiles. The two shook hands, then the older man, in a paternal gesture, put his arm around Jeff's shoulder and escorted him to the door.

Jefferson Foxlove emerged from the offices of the Cudmore agency and walked out onto Madison Avenue with a feeling of self-confidence and euphoria. He felt good because he'd just been hired by an esteemed member of the grand and glorious advertising community. He truly believed at that point that very soon he'd be writing memorable copy and producing ads that would sparkle with honesty, clarity, and purpose. He felt he was on the road to the majestic world of advertising that Ogilvy had described in his book.

Little did the young man realize that Damon Cudmore sneered at the mere mention of Ogilvy's name and he held the ad men of all other agencies in contempt, regarding them as gutless, unimaginative pantywaists. Cudmore was going to teach his newly hired, young protégé to write ads the Cudmore way. It wouldn't be long before Jefferson Foxlove would come to realize that the Cudmore Advertising Agency was a mirror opposite of anything Ogilvy had ever envisioned.

CHAPTER 3

The first six months at the Cudmore Advertising Agency were something of a letdown for Jeff because Cudmore assigned him to all sorts of odds-and-ends jobs. It seemed that Jeff did most everything around the office except the one thing that he really wanted to do—create ads. He did not get to write any ad copy, not one line, not one word, and he was beginning to feel frustrated. After all, he came to Madison Avenue to be an ad man, not a chore boy.

Actually, this was part of Cudmore's diabolical design for the young apprentice. He wanted to hold Jeff at bay for a while; just long enough for the boy to get frustrated and more than a little anxious so he would be chomping at the bit to be a copywriter. When he felt that young Jeff was hungry enough to sit before a word processor, he'd be eager, with his ethics dulled and unmindful of scruples. Then he would hand the boy his first assignment. At that point, young Foxlove would be so keen to accept any assignment without question or reservation.

Just when Jeff was convinced that Cudmore had forgotten him and he would never get a chance to do any writing, the diabolical boss gave him an assignment. When he was first handed the file, Jeff was excited because he thought that at long last he'd have his chance to prove to the world that he had the makings of a first-class advertising man.

He expected that maybe he'd get to write about a luxury car or maybe a high-profile resort or perhaps some exotic perfume; but when he opened the file, he saw that he would have to write an ad for JockPal, an antifungal cream used to cure athlete's foot and treat jock itch, his exhilaration dimmed a little. The realization that he would be writing about a pedestrian product like antifungal cream seemed to take some of the glamour out of the advertising world. Oh well, he had to start somewhere!

For the rest of the afternoon, Jeff sat at his desk doing nothing but thinking. What could he possibly say that would make anyone buy this product? How would David Ogilvy handle this assignment?

Then he remembered what Ogilvy said in his book: "The key to success is to promise the consumer a benefit."

Jeff thought more about the product, it seemed obvious that anyone suffering from the jock-itch rash would be uncomfortable and maybe even in pain. It therefore followed that the sufferer would want to relieve that pain and discomfort and that gave Jeff the magic solution. All he had to do was describe the distress of jock itch then proclaim that JockPal had the medication to cure the malady.

Excited, he roughed out his concept, typed up the copy and printed it out. Then he sketched in a visual and thought of a headline. For the visual he would have a photo of a man clad in gym shorts and tee-shirt sitting on a bench in a club locker room. The man would reflect an anguished expression on his face showing that he was suffering from something.

Hopefully that would capture the reader's attention and make him read the headline which said, "JockPal, the ideal medication to eradicate the suffering caused by jock itch."

Jeff leaned back in his chair with satisfaction. He felt that he'd come up with the perfect solution to a vexing problem. This, he believed, was the kind of straightforward ad copy that David Ogilvy would have created.

With his printed copy and roughly-sketched ad in hand, he rushed around to Cudmore's office to show him his brainstorm. He knocked on Cudmore's door and was bidden to enter. Jeff immediately walked in, marched up to Cudmore's desk and handed him the ad.

Jeff waited while the boss read over his work. He was sure that Cudmore would be delighted with his piece and heap a mound of praise on him, so he was a little dismayed when he didn't respond with immediate enthusiasm. In fact, it turned out to be just the opposite; Cudmore looked up with a sour expression and said, "It doesn't do anything for me. It's dull."

Jeff was deflated and immediately went on the defensive. "Well, I thought it was okay. I mean, it describes the painful rash and says that the product can bring relief. The copy clearly shows how the product will bring benefit to the consumer."

"Yeah, yeah, maybe; but you're pussyfooting around the issue. In advertising you gotta slam-dunk your message so the consumer will sit up and take notice."

"I'm not sure that I understand."

"Well, for instance, you could say something like: when you've got the creeping crud better use JockPal before your balls rot off."

Jeff was aghast and for a moment stood there in stunned silence. Finally, he found his voice. "You really can't say that in an ad, can you? I mean, it's...well, no one would print it, and even if they did, readers would be appalled."

"Okay, so you don't say it exactly like that, but you can suggest it. Sometimes a strong suggestion says more than a lot of namby-pamby words."

"But how can you do that? I mean this is a delicate condition that needs some sort of explanation and tact. You can't just—"

Cudmore cut him off. "Here, let me show you something." He reached into a drawer and pulled out a DVD disc.

"Now this is a spot we did for television. It's a commercial for BanGas pills, they're formulated to eliminate flatulence—that's farting in case you didn't know. Just watch."

Cudmore popped the disc into a player and a nearby wall screen lit up with the BanGas commercial.

The opening scene showed a shot of a woman in a room with a crowd of people behind her. She was in the forefront facing the camera. It was obviously a social occasion with people in the background chatting and sipping cocktails. A voiceover came on to announce that intestinal gas can be uncomfortable and embarrassing. This was quickly followed by a close-up of the woman's face. Her face was contorted in pain and it showed her in obvious discomfort. It was clear this woman was suffering from an uncomfortable accumulation of intestinal gas. Then there was a change in her expression to suggest that she had just done something, although the viewer, at this point, could not be sure what that was.

Then suddenly the camera pulled back to reveal the entire scene and it showed a brownish-blue haze had darkened the entire room. As the brown color deepened and the haze became dense, the expressions on the people's faces turned from cheerful smiles into nauseated grimaces.

The not-so-subtle implication was that the unfortunate woman had just released an atrocious anal gas bomb of such noxious intensity that it threatened to asphyxiate everyone in the room. The people in the room all looked around for the source of the disgusting odor. Some of the people held their noses while others started choking. Meanwhile the woman's face turned three deepening shades of red.

The voiceover then explained how that embarrassing situation could have been avoided if the woman had the foresight to take BanGas pills before going to the party. BanGas would work to absorb the offending flatulence before it could be discharged into the crowd. Everyone could be happy.

Cudmore played and replayed the disc several times while Jeff watched the commercial in total disbelief. He couldn't believe that such a delicate subject as flatulence could be handled with such blatant coarseness. To young Jeff, the commercial seemed offensive in the extreme.

"You see," said Cudmore, oblivious to Jeff's look of distaste, "we used computer enhancement to change the color of the atmosphere in the room to a brownish haze and we used the same technique to add the deep red color to the actress's face. We didn't say anything about cutting a fart or expelling gas; we didn't have to because we made a strong suggestion. We did all of that with a vivid visual and we got our message across without beating around the bush. Pretty clever, huh?"

Jeff was speechless. He looked from the screen back to Cudmore and back again. He couldn't believe what he'd just seen. Cudmore sat back in his chair with a big smile on his face, waiting for his young copywriter to say something.

Finally, Jeff spoke. "Mr. Cudmore, in his book on advertising, David Ogilvy says that you should never run an ad that you wouldn't show to your family. Would you show that to your family?"

"Course I would. Although, the only family I got left is my brother and he's an asshole, so I'd have no qualms about him seeing this. Serve him right if he got offended. Maybe he'd crawl into a hole and hide for the rest of his life."

"But you're not planning on running that commercial on television are you, sir?"

"Already have. It's been on the airwaves for a couple of weeks now. And it's working. We hit a nerve and made a lot of people uncomfortable about being caught at a party when they have a gut full of gas. Yeah, we dropped this little baby on Nagasaki and got ourselves a big mushroom cloud. The client reports that sales of BanGas have really picked up."

"But sir, is it right to do that sort of thing? I mean it seems like the commercial is kind of raunchy; you know, of questionable taste."

"Taste?!" exclaimed Cudmore in obvious contempt for the word. "Let me tell you something about taste, my boy. Something you're probably not aware of. There is no such thing as good or bad taste. That's right. Taste lies in the pocketbook of the consumer; not in the words of some high-minded copywriter working in the office of some hoity-toity ad agency on Madison Avenue."

"But Mr. Cudmore, there must be some people in the community, religious groups, or civic leaders who will object to that kind of ad."

"So what? Who gives a shit what the puritans say? I told you it's the consumer who decides what's good and what's not. If the consumer takes a bite of an ad and decides that it's okay, then he goes out and buys the product. And if enough consumers buy the product, then the sales figures go up and our client becomes a happy camper. And if he's happy, then he pays us to do more ads and that adds money to our bank account. If that happens our agency prospers. Remember, you can't put taste in the bank. Taste is only a matter of what you can get away with. You follow me?"

"I think so," said Jeff with reserve. "But in his book on advertising, David Ogilvy says—"

"Screw Ogilvy," snapped Cudmore. "He's not signing your paycheck. I am. Now go back and write me some copy that seizes the reader by the scruff of the neck, fires a broadside, hits the reader in the guts, and grabs him by the balls. Remember, aim for the jugular."

Jeff walked out of the office shaking his head in disbelief. He wasn't sure if he just got a lesson in copywriting or a brief survey of Anatomy 101.

He went back to his cubicle, crumpled up his ad and tossed it in the trash. Then he plopped into his chair and bit his lip. Somehow this wasn't at all what he expected when he started out in advertising. He stared at the blank screen of his computer and at the same time tried to recall some of the advice and dictums in David Ogilvy's book.

Slowly, however, it dawned on him that this was a whole new ballgame and it wasn't anything like what Ogilvy described in his book. Gradually, Jeff came to realize that in this game, it was Damon Cudmore who was calling the plays and Ogilvy and his high-minded principles didn't count. Jeff came to understand that if he wanted to survive here, he would have to toss intellectual honesty and good taste out the window and do as Cudmore ordered. *Go for the jugular.* And that is exactly what he made up his mind to do.

After mulling it over for the better part of a week, Jeff finally came up with something he thought would fit the Cudmore approach. For the visual he envisioned a close-up of a guy wearing jockey shorts. The jockey shorts were on fire with flames around the crotch area. His headline read, "When you've got a bad case of crotch rot that burns at your vitals down under, use JockPal to put out the fire before it destroys your family jewels."

He sat back and looked at his work on the screen. Well, there it was. It wasn't the kind of ad that he'd want his grandmother to see, but it got the job done—in kind of a heavy-handed way. He printed it out and took it to show Cudmore.

Once again, he found himself standing before the desk, while the Cudmore read over the ad in silence. After a moment of silent reading, Cudmore looked up at Jeff. This time he had a broad smile on his face.

"This is much better. It captures the attention of the reader and tells it like it is. Now you've got the hang of selling a product. Good work!"

And that was it. Jefferson Foxlove was now an adman—but an adman in the Cudmore mold. At that moment Jeff had a vision of David Ogilvy groaning loudly in his grave.

After that, Jeff got one assignment after the other. He never got to write any ads for classy items like cars, high fashion clothes, jewelry, or perfume, because it seemed that the Cudmore Advertising Agency only handled products for personal hygiene and human body problems. So, he wrote one ad after the other for adult diapers, feminine vaginal cream, enemas, douches, mouthwash, deodorants, and diarrhea medicines.

In a very short time, Jeff came to understand that as long as he worked for the Cudmore agency his life would be focused on defecation, constipation, incontinence, halitosis, vaginal itching and body odor. And with that realization, Jeff understood that if he wanted to survive at Cudmore's, he would have to get used to working on the smelly, malodorous side of life.

So, Jeff took the leap into advertising by following in the Cudmore tradition; he threw caution to the winds, held his nose and plunged into the stinko world that Damon Cudmore wallowed in. In less than a year, he became a full-fledged disciple of the master schlock-monger himself, Damon Cudmore; and under Cudmore's tutelage, learned to churn out one sleaze-ball ad campaign after the other. With each assignment he got better and better at composing in the raunchy Cudmore style. All his pieces were blatantly vulgar and tasteless, but nevertheless successful, ad campaigns that made the clients happy and brought money into the bank account of the Cudmore Advertising Agency. Taste then was measured in dollar signs and not in pious accolades.

As a reward for his hard work and his imaginative forays into the realm of utter tastelessness, Jefferson Foxlove was promoted to the position of senior copywriter and for all intents and purposes, it would seem that he was on the road to success. Perhaps he was, but every now and then, at odd moments of solitude, he had his misgivings.

This sort of career wasn't what he set out to do when he graduated from college and set out to get into the ad game and every so often, in brief passing moments, it occurred to him that there had to be more to life than just pushing smelly products and making money without any regard for good taste and integrity.

Yes, he was writing ad copy and churning out one clever campaign after the other; and yes, he was making a good income, and he was now the fair-haired boy of the Cudmore Agency; but was something missing? It was as if there was some deep intrinsic part of himself that wasn't being addressed. He couldn't put his finger on exactly what that something was, but he knew it was somewhere in his makeup.

When he really thought about it, Jeff recognized that he had never completely abandoned values like intellectual honesty, and dedication to craftsmanship, and a deep consideration for quality. He had only smothered them; but he knew that somewhere those ideals were still deep inside of him, but they murmured as a faint voice crying for recognition.

It was faint, but it just wouldn't die, and there were times when this voice did surface unexpectedly. It lasted only a brief moment before it faded. Then he wished that somehow, he could get in touch with that voice and hold it in place so that it would become a permanent part of his life and work. At the same time, he realized that this was a forlorn hope, because even though this nebulous ideal existed deep within him, it was apparent that it would remain forever buried beneath his conscience as long as he worked in the Cudmore Agency and as long as he followed the lead of Damon Cudmore.

He was gradually sinking into the Cudmore morass and at some point, he felt he'd be unable to come to the surface where the air was clean. At that point he would be corrupted beyond redemption and would never be able to realize his hidden, but still cherished values. He was also aware that there was nothing he could do to change the situation—at least not if he wanted to remain in advertising, because now, like it or not, he was officially one of the rams in the Cudmore flock.

CHAPTER 4

It was about this time that Jeff met an aspiring young actress named Dixie Durante. Dixie Durante was her professional name. Her real name was Loretta Farge, but she changed it early in her career because she wanted something that sounded more like a glitzy Hollywood moniker.

Dixie couldn't get many paid acting jobs because she wasn't a particularly good actress—although she didn't know that. She had to make a living by working as a waitress whenever she could; unfortunately, she wasn't very good at that either. In fact, she wasn't very good at anything that required intelligent thought because she was brainless beyond belief. As long as she could stand and show off her beautiful face and gorgeous body she did all right, but when she opened her mouth to say anything, she inadvertently revealed the vast volumes of stupidity that reverberated within her beautiful cranium and eventually turned people off.

Like all hopeful actors, she was forever optimistic, thinking that her big break was just around the corner. She read the trade journals and searched the casting notices on the Internet constantly because she was always on the lookout for a principal part in a movie or a leading role in a play. The only significant movie role she ever had was in the motion picture *Murder on the Docks*. She played the part of a dead body floating in the bay. This was hardly the stuff of memorable histrionics, but Dixie was sure that if she pursued acting, someday she would get noticed and that it would lead to more significant parts.

The only trouble was that she didn't get noticed and there were no forthcoming significant parts, except for one role that came up in an out-of-town production. She auditioned for and got, a role in an original drama that was going to be presented at the Peekskill Playhouse in Peekskill, New York. No one is quite sure how she landed the part but it most likely happened because she was the only woman who came to the audition. This left the director with little choice but to cast Dixie in the female lead role.

The play was written by a young wannabe playwright named Thornton Breastwhite. Breastwhite was not just a playwright, he was a man with a message. He truly believed that scientists experimenting with cloning, stem-cell research, and genetic engineering would eventually make serious mistakes that could threaten the entire human race. With those fears in mind, he sat down and wrote a play reflecting those dire concerns. His play was called, *Science Gone Wrong*, and he hoped that it would serve as a warning to the public as to what could happen if scientific research was not regulated and put under strict control.

Basically, the plot dealt with a scientist who was trying to clone a human being but during the course of his experiments he inadvertently left the window to his laboratory open and this allowed a cloud of toxic gas generated in a nearby landfill to drift in and contaminate his work. The result was that instead of cloning a human being, the scientist created a mutant creature that set out to wreak havoc on the human population.

Dixie was the only out-of-town actor in the play. The other actors were all rank amateurs from around the Peekskill area. Dixie played the part of a young and beautiful socialite, Ruby Van Dweller. In the play, the mutant becomes infatuated with this socialite and contrives to abduct her and take her to his lair in the landfill where he intends to make her his bride.

The part of the mutant was played by Lester Cornby. Cornby was a clerk in the Peekskill hardware store, but had dreams of becoming a serious classical actor. With that object in mind, he had studied Shakespearean acting as well as voice projection, diction, and elocution. In this play, however, he never got to use any of that training because his only lines consisted of various unintelligible, guttural sounds like "Argh! Grahhh!" and "Agghh!"

No one got to see his face—or, for that matter, any other part of his body—because the costume designer dressed him from head to toe in a costume made of shredded plastic bags obtained from the local grocery store. The end result was that Lester Cornby looked a lot like a glistening, white haystack that lumbered about the stage bellowing his limited vocabulary of grunts and groans.

The key scene in the play came when the mutant entered Ruby's bedroom in the middle of the night. Just as he was about to grab the sleeping Ruby and carry her off to the landfill, a courageous investigative reporter, played by another local, dramatic hopeful, Scott Slammer, burst into the room to confront the creature. The mutant attacked the reporter but the intrepid reporter responded by spraying the creature with Lysol, thereby killing it, saving Ruby and ostensibly the rest of the human race.

Dixie delivered her usual lackluster, insipid performance speaking her lines in a relentless monotone devoid of any vocal nuances or emotional inflection. The audience didn't seem to notice how incredibly untalented she was. Perhaps they thought she was demonstrating some sort of avant-garde minimalist acting technique, or perhaps they were all rural rubes who lacked the ability to evaluate talent, or lack of it, when it appeared before them. Whatever the reason, Dixie managed to get through each night without anyone throwing anything at her.

The play was supposed to be a serious drama with urgent, social-political-scientific overtones, but during the first performance the playwright and actors were surprised, and not a little distraught, when the audience responded to their performance at first with snickers and then with peals of laughter. This was hardly the response that anyone in the cast was expecting. At the end of the performance, however, the audience rose to give the entire cast a standing ovation.

Two days later, there was a review of the performance in the local paper, the *Peekskill Peephole*. The review said the play, *Science Gone Wrong*, was hysterically funny and that the playwright, Thornton Breastwhite

WEREWOLF ON MADISON AVENUE

showed rare talent as a farceur. The critic went on to say that the play was an imaginative burlesque of the old monster movies of the fifties.

Needless to say, this was not the kind of reaction that Breastwhite had anticipated when he wrote the play, and he regarded the review and the audience response with consternation. At that point he decided that the theater-going public and the critics were too unsophisticated to appreciate serious drama with an urgent message, and he vowed never to write another play. He made that declaration before the entire cast of *Science Gone Wrong*, and he was rather dismayed to find that no one in the group said anything to try and dissuade him from his solemn vow.

While the play was running Dixie hoped that maybe an important producer or director would be in the audience, see her perform, and hopefully recognize her imagined star quality offering her a big part. However, that never happened so she came back to Manhattan to pursue her moribund acting career. As luck would have it, she got a call from an agent who sent her to audition for a part in a commercial being produced by the Cudmore Advertising Agency.

The commercial was for The American Prune Council. Jeff Foxlove wrote the spot to show consumers how they could achieve regularity by eating a dish of stewed prunes every morning.

Dixie was cast as an extra playing the part of a prune. She appeared wearing a prune costume and had no lines. Her role consisted of swaying in the background with a bunch of other prune-players while the featured actor looked into the camera with a pained expression and complained about his chronic constipation.

Jeff was on set to make sure that everything was going according to plan, but as he watched the filming, he realized that the commercial message wasn't getting across with the force that he intended. At that point, he decided to add a line and he enlisted Dixie to come forward and say, "Eat me and I'll give you all the right moves."

Dixie was elated because she got an upgrade, and Jeff was satisfied because he felt that this simple addition grabbed the viewer by the scruff of the neck and drove the message of blissful regularity home to the consumer.

Because of her change in status, from background extra to one-liner, Dixie was able to join the Screen Actors' Guild. The Screen Actors' Guild, aka SAG, is the major union to which all the movie stars belong. When she joined the union and got her SAG card, Dixie truly believed that she was on her way to fame and fortune in the movie industry and that it was only a matter of time before the major studios would call to tell her that she was to be cast in the lead of an upcoming movie with Tom Cruise as her co-star.

Alas for poor Dixie, the calls from the Hollywood producers did not materialize. In fact, she still found it difficult to get a part in anything. It looked like her career was going nowhere fast. At that point Dixie remembered Jefferson Foxlove and she thought that if he helped her once, then maybe he could do it again. So, she called him at the Cudmore Agency.

"Hello. Is Mr. Foxlove in?"

"Yes, this is he."

"Mr. Foxlove, this is Dixie Durante. You probably don't remember me but I was in your commercial for The American Prune Council. I played a prune in the background, but you were nice enough to give me a line to speak."

"Oh yes, of course I remember you. I remember you very well." That was a lie, he had only a vague recollection of the prune actress, but he said otherwise to be nice to her.

"Well, Mr. Foxlove, I just called to tell you how much I enjoyed performing for you; and I want you to know that I would like to work with you again sometime."

"Thank you, Miss Durante, that's very nice to hear."

At this point in the conversation there was a lingering pause. Jeff waited to hear if Dixie had anything more to say. Dixie waited, hoping that Jeff would take the hint and maybe offer her a part in an upcoming commercial, but he didn't say anything more so she continued.

"Well, I was wondering if maybe you might have something in the works that I would be right for. I should tell you that I can sing as well as act."

"That's good to know, but the truth is that I don't have anything at the moment. I am, however, working on a commercial for a toilet bowl cleaning product. We still have to get client approval for the concept, but if it flies, then we'll probably go before the cameras sometime next month."

"Do you think there would be a part in it for me? Maybe a speaking role?"

"Well, there is only one speaking role and that will be the part of a block of deodorizing-scrubbing cleanser. I'm afraid that will have to go to a man because we think that a man will better convey the strength of the cleansing product."

"Oh!" said Dixie, clearly disappointed.

"But there might be a role for you in the background. We need a number of background actors to play the effervescent bubbles that dance around the brown ring at the water line of the toilet bowl."

"Well, that sounds good," said Dixie.

She tried to sound upbeat, but the truth is that this was not the kind of role that she had envisioned when she called him; but still it was a part and if she did get cast then she would at least appear on camera and get paid for it. This could be a way of keeping her face before the public until her big break came. She said she'd love to do it and she hoped that he would keep her in mind when the time came for casting the commercial. He said he would.

As she clicked off the phone she realized that for the time being at least, Jeff Foxlove was her one and only key to fame. So, she decided to cultivate his friendship. She called him again later in the week. Then she called him during the following weeks, finally every day.

She contrived to stage an accidental meeting with him when he was coming out of his office. After that, she made sure that she saw him frequently. Pretty soon they began dating. When they were together she tried always to purr and coo around him and snuggle up to him so that he would want her for his girlfriend. Dixie Durante might not have been a competent performer on the stage but in the romance department she was aces and as such, she was able to make young Jeff become infatuated with her.

It seemed like love to him; because when they were together they petted and cuddled, Dixie praised and flattered him and sometimes they slept together. All that added up to love didn't it? Well, maybe, but somehow Jeff had the feeling that there must be more to love than just physical pleasure. There had to be something else and that something else, whatever it was, just wasn't present in their relationship.

Maybe it was something intellectual. They had a good, physical-sexual relationship but they never really talked about anything. Dixie seemed incapable of sustained conversation. She exhibited the attention span of a butterfly and the intelligence of a newt.

But as he reflected on their times together, he felt that there was even something greater, even beyond the physical and the intellectual; something deeper, something spiritual that he was at a loss to describe. No matter how much he thought about it, he couldn't pin down the source of his frustration. All he knew was that he was missing some sort of key ingredient that he needed to make him feel really happy.

This was something that he couldn't talk about and he kept his inner feelings to himself, so no one suspected there was anything amiss in Jeff's life. Indeed, the casual observer looking at Jeff would say that he had it all and that the various parts of Jeff's life had come together perfectly.

He had a career with good pay, a beautiful girlfriend, and a nice apartment. What more could a young man want? What indeed? That was the question that troubled Jeff every now and then. He was aware of what he had achieved but he also knew that he wanted something more out of life. But what was that something? That was the big question and now his problem was, try as he might, he couldn't find the answer to that vexing inquiry.

CHAPTER 5

Jefferson Foxlove continued working at the Cudmore Advertising Agency for the next two years. During that time, he churned out copy, developed ads campaigns, pushed products, and pitched crap, relentlessly working five, sometimes six, days a week, often working overtime, and all without a break. During this time, even though it seemed that he was a very successful young man, those inner doubts of his, those vague questions about what he wanted to do in life, continued to plague him.

It was then that he decided that he needed a break. It was time for a vacation. He figured that what he needed was a chance to get away, to go someplace quiet, chill out a little, and maybe, at the same time, explore his inner psyche, consider his options and possibly plan a strategy for his future. Maybe a little solitude, far away from the rat race of Madison Avenue was what he needed to refocus and find a greater purpose in life.

He didn't know exactly where he wanted to go, but he thought that it should be someplace distant from New York City, someplace completely different, someplace where he could smell clean fresh air, feel a mild breeze on his face, see the clear blue sky, and maybe even swim in the salty breakers. After looking over a number of travel brochures and talking to several travel agents, Jeff decided that he would like to visit the Yucatan peninsula.

Now Jeff had never been to the Yucatan; but judging from the many brochures he looked at, it seemed nice—an ideal place to visit. It looked like it offered all the pleasures that he wanted in a vacation spot: warm and sunny climate, lush green vegetation, blue skies, quaint villages, and fantastic Mayan ruins.

Moreover, he assumed that it would be a place unspoiled by the crass commercialism and materialism that had become a major part of his life for the past few years. He would leave the first of the month for three weeks. What Jefferson did not know when he made his travel plans was that this vacation would prove to be the turning point in his life, and not in a way that he could ever imagine.

Maybe it was his imagination, but it seemed to him that time had slowed to a glacial pace while he wallowed in the day-to-day world of human body problems handled with tasteless advertising. Whatever the cause, it seemed that, some days, time almost came to a complete stop. But the days and hours did move along, however slowly, and eventually the first of the month did arrive.

Jeff took a car to Newark International Airport, checked in and boarded a plane. When all the passengers were on board and seated in place, the flight attendants closed and locked the door, and the plane taxied to the end of the runway and waited. And waited. Once again it seemed that time had come to a standstill. Jeff wondered if he was destined to spend his vacation sitting at the end of a runway. The plane did eventually take off, and as it gained altitude, Jeff knew at last that he was really on his way. Goodbye drab, hectic New York; hello to relaxation in the sunny tropics.

The plane flew to the island of Cozumel. Jeff had planned to spend the first few days of his holiday on this tiny island. After that, he would ferry across to the Yucatan.

When he arrived at the Cozumel airport, he took a cab to town and booked a room in a hotel. He spent the next few days wandering about the town, exploring the shops, tasting the local cuisine, buying a few souvenirs. One afternoon, he visited the local museum. On another day, he managed to get in some snorkeling. Then, when he decided that he'd seen about all that Cozumel had to offer, he packed his bag, checked out of the hotel and took the ferry across the water to the Yucatan peninsula.

The ferry landed at the dock on the mainland, Jeff found a bus service nearby and he boarded an old bus that drove from the coast into the interior of the peninsula. As the antiquated bus traveled along the crude back roads, Jeff looked out the window at the lush, verdant countryside and he was filled with a sense of wonder. This was a far cry from the concrete and brick canyons of Manhattan, from the glass and steel office towers of Madison Avenue. The sight of the beautiful panorama and the atmosphere of unhurried tranquility, a life totally different from the dog-eat-dog world of advertising as he was living it, gave him a sense of contentment and serenity that he hadn't experienced before.

There seemed to be a purity about the land, a fresh wholesomeness that was unspoiled by the crass commercialism that drove the environment that he lived and worked in. This was a decided change from the world that he was used to, and he found that now he could relax, enjoy himself, and throw off big city cares and concerns he'd endured for so long. As the bus penetrated deeper into the interior, Jeff became increasing eager to find a stopping place so he could get out, wander about the land, take pictures of the bucolic surroundings and at the same time, get a real feel for the country.

The bus stopped to discharge and pick up passengers at villages and small towns along the way. Most of these places had little to offer the wandering tourist, so Jeff did not disembark. Eventually, however, the bus came to a small village that had a few shops, a cantina and a tiny hotel. When the bus stopped in this tiny hamlet, Jeff knew instinctively that this was it. This was the village where he wanted to stay for the next few days. This was the place where he would wander about, explore the Yucatan and soak up the atmosphere of the jungle.

Jeff got off the bus and checked into the hotel. The hotel didn't have much in the way of amenities, but it did have running water—although Jeff wasn't sure of its origin. His room was small, simple, and Spartan to the extreme, but it was clean and neat and had a large window that let in copious amounts of warm sunlight. Jeff threw his bag on the bed and walked over to the window. As he stood there and gazed out at the mountains in the distance, he noticed something strange. There were bars on the window. He found that curious and wondered what they were there for.

Jeff slept soundly that night. The next day, feeling refreshed and full of life, he decided that he wanted to explore the local jungle. He inquired at the hotel for someone in the village who might be willing to serve as a guide. The hotel clerk suggested a local man who was trustworthy and who knew the territory. When Jeff agreed, the clerk sent a messenger to fetch a man named Miguel.

Miguel came to the hotel to meet Jeff, and after settling on a modest fee, he agreed to take Jeff into the jungle. They arranged for the cantina to make up some food and drink that they could take on their hike, and then they set off into the bush with Miguel leading the way.

They began walking along a simple path that headed through the bush and up the mountainside. Almost immediately Jeff was enthralled by everything in sight: the mountain trail, the birds in the trees, the bushes, the flowers, and even the strange insects. He stopped periodically to take pictures of all these new, novel things. He caught glimpses of the trees and flowers and any birds or lizards that would hold still long enough for a photo.

After walking all morning and part of the afternoon, the two reached a clearing on top of the mountain and they stopped there to sit and eat their lunch. They ate mostly in silence with Jeff getting up occasionally to move about and take pictures.

Finally, after an hour had elapsed, Miguel spoke.

"Well, it is getting late and we should be starting back."

"Why? There's still plenty of sunlight."

"Yes, Señor, but the sun goes down quickly here, and it is not good to be out in this jungle at night."

"Guess it gets pretty dark here, huh?"

"Usually it does, Señor, although tonight it will be lighter because there will be a full moon out."

"Really? Boy, I'd like to see that. It must be beautiful with all this country lit up by moon glow."

"No Señor, believe me, you do not want to be up here tonight. Not tonight when the full moon is up."

"Why not?" asked Jeff. "What's so bad about the moon? I should think that with the light of the full moon, it would be easy to find your way about. You would be able to see the trail so you couldn't get lost and I imagine it would probably be very peaceful up here."

"I am not worried about getting lost, Señor. And it is not peaceful. You can meet strange things out here at night, things that are mean, ugly and trouble."

"What exactly? You mean like maybe a jaguar or a mountain lion or something like that?"

"No, Señor, those animals will not come to this part of the jungle at night. They know better."

Jeff looked at Miguel. This conversation was taking a strange turn and he wondered what the guide was alluding to.

"Jaguars and mountain lions know better! What do you mean by that? What is it they know? You make it sound like they're afraid of something."

"There are creatures here that run in the jungle after dark. They are afraid of these things."

Jeff was starting to get annoyed because he couldn't grasp what Miguel was alluding to. There was clearly something on the guide's mind, something that he seemed to think was unsafe, but his answers were so vague and evasive that Jeff couldn't get a hint of what is was.

"What sort of creatures are you talking about? What kind could frighten jaguars and lions?"

"There are strange, wild creatures that come out at night, under the light of the full moon."

"I still don't understand what you're talking about. Have you seen any of these creatures yourself? I mean with your own eyes?"

"No, Señor, people who see these creatures do not live to tell about them."

"Then how do you know that they exist?"

"I have heard many stories, Señor, from people in my village."

"Oh," said Jeff somewhat scornfully, "so that's what's bothering you. You're afraid of stories, rumors and superstition. Your fears aren't based on anything that you know directly or have come in contact with. You're only afraid of what people have told you."

Miguel shrugged. "That is so, but some of the people in village do know what happens here and we have learned to believe in their stories. We know them to be true."

Jeff looked hard at Miguel. Surely these tales of creatures of the night were all a lot of nonsense. Miguel had never seen any of these strange beings. This was clearly a classic manifestation of the old Chinese proverb; *three men make a tiger.*

Thus, if one man tells you that he has seen a tiger in the marketplace, you dismiss the tale as a figment of the man's imagination. If two men tell you that they've seen a tiger in the marketplace, then you begin to wonder if there might be something to the tale. Now if three men tell you that they've seen that tiger, then you really have to believe them because you have three witnesses and three men can't be wrong. Anyway, that's the theory behind the proverb.

But Jeff knew better—at least he thought he did. He recognized this type of reasoning as the *bandwagon effect*, and he was acquainted with it because he'd used the technique in many of his advertising campaigns. It's simple: convince the consumer that enough people buy and use a certain product and he will buy it because he believes that is what the majority does and he doesn't want to be any different from the gang.

Miguel was clearly a victim of this effect. His entire village believed in strange mythological creatures so Miguel felt compelled to believe in them too, simply because everyone else did. In a small village you have to go with the pack because there is no room for individual thought. It was herding instinct that made him a believer, nothing else.

Well, the more Jeff thought about this whole situation, the more he became convinced that someone had to take a stand and show Miguel and these simple villagers that there really was no "beast in the moonlit night," and as Jeff thought about the situation he decided that the person to debunk the baseless myth was himself.

"Miguel," he said, "I've decided that I'm going to stay here and watch the moon come up. I think it would be beautiful to see this glorious country in the light of the full moon. I would imagine that the mountains and jungles in moonlight would be absolutely breathtaking."

Miguel was horror struck. "No, Señor, please you do not want to do that. You don't know what you are saying. You must not stay here. You will be in great danger."

Jeff smiled at Miguel's superstitious fear.

"No, Miguel, I've made up my mind. This is what I want to do. You're welcome to stay with me if you want to. It looks like we have enough food for both of us to have a supper up here. But whether you remain or not, I am going to stay up here through the night."

Miguel vehemently shook his head. "No, I cannot do that. I am sorry Señor, I will not stay here with you. I cannot do that. I have a wife and family, and I must think of them. The sun will be going down soon, and I must leave now if I am to get back to the village before dark. Please come with me."

"No, Miguel. I told you, my mind is made up. I'm staying up here. If you feel that you must go, then go; but I'm staying here, with or without you."

"Señor," Miguel pleaded, "you do not understand. Trust me, it is too dangerous for you to remain here."

"Miguel, that's where you're wrong. I do understand. I understand that you are all afraid of shadows in the night. It's all superstitious claptrap, nothing more; and I intend to stay and prove that. Now you go home if you want. I'll see you in the morning."

"I hope so, Señor."

Miguel shook his head sadly, then rose, and started walking away. Just before he reached the edge of the clearing he turned back to look at Jeff. He looked back this one last time to see if maybe Jeff was going to change his mind; but he saw the young man standing there with unshakable resolve. The guide saw that nothing could budge the young American. Miguel shook his head sadly then started to walk by himself down the mountain along the rugged path. And all the time that he was walking back to his village he pictured the crazy American who was risking certain death just to see the light of the full moon on a few plants. He was convinced that he would never see that man again.

CHAPTER 6

With Miguel gone, Jeff was alone on the mountaintop, surrounded by a wall of dense, green vegetation with the darkening blue sky overhead. This was an isolation and solitude that was peaceful, relaxing, restful. He savored a tranquility unlike any he had ever experienced before. He looked around at the wall of trees, bushes, and lush vegetation surrounding him, and he listened to the sounds of the birds and insects in the jungle. Jeff felt a sense of exhilaration as though he were on a higher plane of existence more vital than any he'd ever experienced before. He felt as though he were at one with nature, a primitive existence. It could be here, on this night, that he would finally connect with his true inner self.

He took pictures of everything around him. Then after he felt that he had captured everything of significance, he sat down on a rock and he pulled out some of the remaining food from his pack and ate it. As the sun started to go down, the warm rays of remaining light changed the sky overhead to a beautiful, golden-red canvas. Jeff sat there on that mountaintop and looked all around at the dense jungle and at the gorgeous, majestic sky overhead. This was nature at its most beautiful and he was glad that he'd made the decision to stay behind and savor it all.

But soon the sun dropped below the horizon and the light began to fade. The trees, plants and flowers lost their color and definition, appearing as vague forms of muted shades of gray. Now the world didn't seem as warm and friendly as before, and doubts began to creep into Jeff's consciousness. He began to wonder if he made the right decision. Miguel said that night came on quickly in the jungle and as the darkness encircled him, Jeff saw that the guide was right. In less than an hour, Jeff was surrounded by darkness, and it was a darkness blacker and more dense, opaque, and forbidding than he'd ever experienced. What's more, there was no way to cut through that darkness, because Jeff realized that he neglected to bring a flashlight. He felt as if he'd suddenly gone blind.

As the night fell, the jungle came alive with all sorts of creatures, totally hidden from sight, singing, chirping, squawking. These were sounds unlike any that he'd ever heard and he had the sudden awareness that he was a solitary human on a strange mountain, surrounded by unknown creatures in a black, noisy jungle in the middle of the Yucatan. He was thousands of miles from his safe and familiar home and he felt alone, so terribly alone and vulnerable; and there was no way out.

But then the moon started to rise. It was a beautiful, bright, full moon. As it climbed higher into the heavens, it lit up the sky and made the clouds glow. It bathed the clearing where he stood in a kind of mystical light that illuminated the plants and the trees, giving them a surreal shimmering luster. The ground was suddenly visible again albeit in a ghostly light. Jeff looked about him and was captivated by the majesty of the jungle world, illuminated by the mystical light of the full moon.

Now that he could see what was around him, his fear of being alone faded and his confidence returned. Once again, he was glad that he had stayed behind because now he was a witness to this exquisite world, a hidden world, one that few other people had ever experienced. It was as if he were a solitary spectator to nature's secret, spectacular show.

He took out his camera and started to take more pictures, hoping that he could capture some of the awesome beauty of the surreal, moonlit night. Jeff became so engrossed in picture-taking that he failed to notice the many creatures of the jungle night had become mute. Gradually, all of the sounds diminished and faded until a quiet, deathly stillness pervaded.

Jeff was so occupied with his camera that he didn't notice how quiet everything had become. It was only when he looked up and searched about for something else to photograph that he became aware of the stillness and eerie silence. He thought it strange that all the creatures of the night had suddenly and mysteriously lost their voices. He waited and listened, assuming that in a moment the sounds of the jungle would start up again, but they didn't. Everything remained deathly quiet except for the slight rustling of leaves by a slight breeze.

Jeff stood in place, motionless, just waiting and listening, straining his ears to capture the sound of anything that might be about in the dense bush. He stood there like a statue for the longest time. He waited and listened, but the only sound he could detect was the sound of his breathing. Then after what seemed like earth without time, there came a sound. At first it was very faint.

He continued to stand without moving, just listening, straining to define the sound and pinpoint where it was coming from. Seconds passed and the faint, subtle sound became more obvious. It was the sound of rustling leaves. What was causing it? The breeze had died. Something else was causing it.

Remaining motionless, Jeff strained to capture every nuance of the sound. It seemed to come from something moving about through the vegetation. He continued to stand there motionless, listening without stirring. The sound was getting louder. Something was moving through the bush, and that something, whatever it was, was coming closer.

As he stood there on that lonely mountaintop, listening to the sounds of an unknown something moving, Jeff recalled Miguel's words about the mysterious creatures of the night that move through the jungle under the light of the full moon. Those words, those images, now seemed to mean something and he felt the icy grip of fear enveloping him.

He looked about for someplace to go, someplace to hide, some tree to climb; but there was nothing. There was no way out. No place to run to, no place to hide. He was all by himself, exposed to the wilds, at the mercy of the creatures of the night. He didn't even have a defense

He tried to get a grip on his emotions. These were typical sounds of the bush. That's all they were, sounds, nothing more. After all, he hadn't really seen anything. Most likely his fears were totally groundless. That's what he told himself, but this rationale did not work, and he felt his apprehension growing.

Miguel's words echoed within his mind and Jeff realized that he had made a mistake, perhaps a fatal one, by staying up on the mountain by himself. He decided that maybe it was time to beat a hasty retreat and take the path back down the mountain. Run and get out of the clearing, and away from the phantom creature as soon as possible.

But as he looked around him, Jeff couldn't see any way out; even with the full moon it was still too dark to see where the path was. He knew that it was somewhere on his left side, but the light wasn't bright enough and he couldn't see any discernible gaps in the wall of vegetation. Everywhere was an impenetrable barrier of bushes, trees, dense brush and opaque shadows that concealed the path. He didn't know if they might be hiding things that were forbidding and dangerous. Better to stay in the clearing then, where he had open space around him.

Jeff told himself that he was being silly. He was letting his imagination overcome reason. What was there to fear from bushes and trees and things that go bump in the night? Maybe this mysterious creature, if there really was one, was more afraid of him than he was of it.

For a fleeting moment he almost believed his own rationale. Then he heard the sounds of movement in the bushes again, and he knew that there really was something out there. Somewhere in the thick bush and it seemed to be coming closer. Up till now, the thing, whatever it was, had no shape or form. It was just a sound of rustling branches. Then he heard a low, guttural growl and the mysterious thing suddenly took on an added dimension.

Jeff could feel his flesh grow cold and suddenly he knew what people meant by chills running up and down the spine. There he was on a lonely mountaintop with some nebulous creature lurking in the shadows and he had no place to run—no place to hide. He took a step, leaned forward and peered into the deep, black wall of shadow. To his sudden horror, he saw two bright, incandescent orbs in the underbrush; and Jeff Foxlove knew he was looking at another pair of eyes. The creature, whatever it was, had found him and was looking back at him.

For a moment all was quiet, all was stillness. Jeff tried to move his feet but they seemed glued to the ground. He was paralyzed with fear. He could feel his heart pounding and the hot blood pulsing in his ears

Thus, for one long moment, it was as if time had ceased to exist and Jeff silently prayed to heaven. He prayed that the creature, whatever thing it might be, would only be curious and as soon as it had its visual fill, it would continue on its way. Then, without warning, the bushes suddenly parted and a darkly vague, undefined shape sprang from the darkness and attacked the helpless adman-turned-adventurer, Jefferson Foxlove.

The attack happened so quickly that Jeff didn't have time to duck or even put up his arms for protection. All he knew was that something had lunged at him and struck him with the force of a pile-driver. It knocked the wind out of him and sent him to the ground flat on his back. It all happened so quickly that there was no time to get his bearings. The beast was on top of him, a creature with savage eyes, hairy, with incredibly strong limbs.

Jeff tried to fight back. He was going by instinct, wriggling in the dirt, swinging his arms, trying desperately to push off the strange, savage animal. Everything was happening so fast and they were thrashing about so violently that he couldn't make out a distinct form; but he could feel the hot breath and gooey saliva on his face. And there were moments when he could see the creature's long, white fangs flash in the moonlight.

The savage creature had arms like a man, not legs like a big cat. Jeff felt claws dig into his arms and the creature lunged, sinking its long fangs into his shoulder near his neck. The pain was intense, but Jeff continued to fight for his life suddenly knowing that he was losing the struggle.

In desperation he reached out and grabbed a handful of dirt from the ground. He flung it into the creature's face. This sudden, spontaneous action caught the beast off guard. It recoiled, reared back and brought its paws up to its face, rubbing its eyes. Jeff was momentarily free from the clutches of his feral assailant. He arched his body upward with a sudden push and knocked the beast off of him. The creature was off balance and Jeff seized the opportunity to make a lunge headlong into the bush. He broke through the leaves and branches and plunged forward, crawling, running, moving any way that he was able. Then, without warning, he found that the ground had unexpectedly dropped out from under him falling off into a steep slope. Suddenly, he was tumbling through the air. Falling, falling, until he hit the ground with a thud.

When he hit the ground, he started rolling and flipping down the side of the mountain through underbrush and over bare ground. His plummeting body gathered momentum and he continued down, down, until at last the ground flattened out. Jeff rolled into a body of shallow water.

He lay there flat on his back, weak, spent feeling incredible pain. He knew that he was wounded and probably bleeding profusely. He truly believed that he was about to die. All his strength was gone. All he could do was lie there and wait for the inevitable end which was probably not far off. His thoughts gradually faded and he lapsed into unconsciousness at the foot of the mountain in a stream of water, under the light of the full moon.

CHAPTER 7

Sunlight was just creeping through the trees when Jeff awoke the next morning. When he opened his eyes, his pupils were struck by the morning sun. When he raised his arm to shield his eyes, he felt a shock of intense pain shoot through his arm and shoulder. The rest of his body was stiff and sore. He was groggy and it felt like his brain was barely functioning; so, he lay there for the longest time, without moving, without stirring.

He was trying desperately to make his brain function, to take stock of his situation, and inventory his body parts. Slowly his mind started to operate, albeit on a very fundamental level. After a few minutes, he had consciousness enough to realize that he was lying flat on his back with half of his body on dry land—the other half in a shallow stream. It occurred to him that whatever creature had attacked him was gone. He was slowly bringing his mind back online.

Where exactly was he, and how did he get here? Slowly, incrementally, his mind began to wake up and it evoked images of the events that had brought him to here and now. There was the small hotel in the Yucatan, and hiking up the mountain with a guide. Gradually the pieces of the previous day began to fall into place. He recalled reaching the summit of the mountain and coming into the clearing. Then he remembered the night before of his being alone on the mountain top in the light of the full moon. That much was vivid. But what came after that?

Jeff tried hard to remember. Then suddenly the shock of recognition hit him like a thunderbolt. The experience of the strange beast-creature lunging out of the jungle, and the violent struggle that followed all came back to him, and then the horror of the previous night engulfed him. He sat bolt-upright and looked frantically around. But as he surveyed his surroundings, all seemed remarkably peaceful and quiet.

It was a bright, sun-lit morning. Birds squawked above. A slight breeze brushed the shrubs, and some grasshoppers whirred along the ground. All was apparently tranquil and serene. Whatever happened the previous night was over and done with; today was a new day.

Sitting upright, with his mind more or less functioning, Jeff examined his body. He reached over to his shoulder and felt the muscles; he explored his skin for the gaping wound and torn flesh that he thought was there. To his surprise there was no evidence of any damage. How could that be?

He looked at his limbs and felt around his torso. His examination revealed only a few bumps, bruises, and scratches. As far as he could tell, his body seemed to be in normal working order, a little the worse for wear, but still functioning and still in one piece. He was dirty and disheveled, his clothes were ripped and torn, but that was the extent of damage.

Next, he started to ponder his present whereabouts and how he came to be where he was. Obviously, the events of the previous night brought him here. But what were those events and what exactly had happened the night before? Jeff continued to sit there, oblivious to the fact that his body still lay half submerged in the shallow stream. He rested his head in his hands and tried hard to think, but reconstructing the events of the previous night proved to be arduous because his brain remained tired and groggy.

As he pondered his situation, it seemed that he was getting two different pictures—his mind was telling him one thing, his body another. His mind was trying to reconstruct a nightmare that flashed vague, terrifying images of a strange beast springing out of the darkness and attacking. His tired brain replayed the violent scene of a struggle in which that savage, mysterious creature overpowered him, clawed at his flesh and sank its fangs into his neck.

But if that really happened, then why wasn't he wounded? Why were there no gashes or slashes anywhere on his body? And where was the creature now? His body was now offering him empirical evidence that the attack never happened.

He began thinking it was only a wild hallucination of some sort. But what would have caused such a thing? After all, he had never had such a vivid, terrifying dream before. Why now?

After thinking about it, he concluded that maybe the food prepared for him the day before had something to do with his state of mind. Possibly he wasn't used to the ingredients and some sort of opioid, a rare indigenous spice or root perhaps, had taxed his digestive tract and affected his nervous system. Maybe something wasn't cooked properly and had gone bad, giving him a case of food poisoning that had affected his mind as well as his body.

If there really was a beast why didn't it finish him off? And why wasn't he all torn up? Why was he still alive? Whatever happened, whether a nightmare or an actual struggle, it happened the night before and now it was over. All that was behind him and it was time to abandon the wilderness and try to get back to his hotel.

Rising and standing was difficult and required great effort because his body was still aching and his muscles were weak; but after a few minutes, he was able to master his balance, and when he felt sufficiently steady, he started to walk.

He wasn't exactly sure of his bearings but he looked back at the looming mountain and saw that it continued as a range that branched off to his right. The village and his hotel must be in the other direction, so he turned left and started walking. Presently he came to a gravelly road. Judging by the direction the sun had traveled, Jeff figured that the road ran from north to south and he guessed that the village should be somewhere toward the north.

Jeff turned onto the road and followed it in what he thought was a northerly direction. By now the sun was at its zenith, and it beamed down on him with an unyielding intensity. He was hot, tired, hungry and thirsty, but he continued walking, praying that he would get to the town before he collapsed.

Jeff moved mechanically like a robot on automatic pilot, devoid of feeling and sensation. His mind seemed barely conscious, not functioning entirely and without any awareness of time.

After walking for what seemed like forever, he looked at the horizon and his heart felt a small burst of joy, for he perceived that his village was in the distance. He managed to find a little extra strength to quicken his pace, and soon the village which was a wispy image a few moments previous, now came into focus.

Jeff realized to his immense relief that he had done it; he had made the right assumptions and taken the correct course. The village with his hotel, warm bed, cool shower, and food—delicious, nourishing food—was just a short distance away.

It wasn't long before he was limping through the streets of the village, and as he walked, he could see from the corner of his eye that the village people stopped whatever they were doing to stare at him. They looked at him as if were a corpse risen from the grave. This scrutiny didn't bother Jeff; he knew he was dirty and disheveled with torn and filthy clothes. He knew that he must look a sight.

He'd been gone the whole night and day and reappeared like a ghost; it was only natural that they would be curious about him. But Jeff was in no mood to stop and satisfy their curiosity. All he wanted at that moment was a heap of tasty food, then back to his hotel where he could shower and collapse into bed.

CHAPTER 8

Jeff walked to the cantina. He was filthy and he was ravenously hungry. After all, he hadn't eaten anything since the night before when he'd munched on those morsels in his backpack. He walked into the small cantina and looked around. There were no patrons so he had the choice of any of the four tables in the place.

Jeff sat down and looked for the waiter. The waiter was on the other side of the room. He saw Jeff come in, but he didn't move. He just stood in place, looking a Jeff, watching him, studying him as if he expected something to happen. Jeff beckoned to him and he came over; Jeff ordered chicken with rice and beans, and a bottle of beer. It wasn't long before the waiter came back with a bottle of beer and a glass, then he went to the kitchen and returned with a large plate with a half chicken and a heaping mound of red beans and yellow rice. Jeff immediately started to dig in. The food provided a nourishing relief to his famished body.

Jeff was so engrossed in feeding his face that at first, he failed to notice that men from the village entered the cantina and took up positions at the nearby tables. When Jeff finally looked up from his plate he saw all of the tables around him were occupied, but curiously, no one was eating. Instead they were all looking intently at him. In the forefront of the group, sitting directly opposite him, was Miguel.

"Hello Miguel. Is everything all right?"

"That is what we came to ask you, Señor. Is everything all right with you?"

"Sure, everything is fine with me. Couldn't be better."

"But you spent the night up on the mountain, in the jungle."

"I sure did."

"And what happened?"

"Nothing. Not one blessed thing happened."

Miguel looked at him warily.

"But the people saw you when you walked into the village today. They said you were dirty and that your clothes were torn. You are still soiled. Something must have happened."

"Oh that," said Jeff in an off-hand manner, "yeah, well, I can explain that. You see on top of the mountain I tripped and fell over and then rolled down the side of the mountain. I landed on flat land at the very bottom on the bank of a stream. I got some bumps and bruises but no major injuries. So, as you can see, it was no big deal."

Miguel paused to take in that explanation. He looked around at the other villagers. They exchanged glances but no one said anything; it was obvious that something was bothering them. Miguel continued.

"But Señor, I do not understand when you say you tripped. How did that happen? What was it that you tripped over, and what was it that made you fall from the mountain?"

"I don't really know. I mean it was dark and I couldn't see much and… well, I tripped; probably on a vine or something. Does it really matter? After all, as I said, it wasn't a big deal."

Miguel, however, wasn't so easily placated. "But Señor if you had just tripped, you would have fallen down and stayed there. But you tripped and rolled down that whole, big mountain. You must have been moving fast in order to do that. And your clothes were torn. How can that be?"

"Well maybe I was moving. You see, I had this crazy dream…it was more like a kind of strange hallucination…it must have been something

I ate that caused it…anyway I became disorientated and I guess I jumped about and lost my footing. Then I rolled down the mountain. I keep telling you that it was nothing to get worked up about."

Miguel's eyes narrowed. "Señor, you say you had a dream. Were you sleeping? Tell us about this dream. What did you dream about?"

"I don't see that it makes much difference, but if you really want to know, I dreamt that I was being attacked by some sort of animal. I guess something in the food, or maybe your suggestion about creatures in the night, put those thoughts into my head. Anyway, in my dream this creature jumped out of the bushes at me and clawed and bit me. But as I said before, it was a dream; it didn't amount to anything."

Now Jeff was trying to tell all of this in a casual, nonchalant manner assuming that he could dismiss the matter as being inconsequential; but as he described his dream he could see that the men around him did not take his narrative lightly. Instead they remained serious, wary, and skeptical. When he got to the part about an animal attacking him, there was an audible gasp from the spectators. They exchanged glances and knowing nods as if they knew something that he did not.

After he had finished, there was a long, pregnant pause. Finally, Miguel spoke, "Señor, what you had was not a dream. It really did happen. You were attacked by the creature of the night."

The other men nodded in agreement.

"That's ridiculous. It didn't really happen. It couldn't have, and I can prove it."

Jeff leaned back and opened his shirt. He extended his arms.

"There, look at that. There are no marks on me. If some beast had attacked me, you'd expect to see claw marks, scratches and tears, but there's nothing. Nothing at all. I haven't been harmed in any way. See, I'm whole. That proves it was only a dream."

Miguel shook his head. "No, that only proves something else. You were attacked, and there were wounds. But by the morning they were healed. That is because you are now one of them. You are now a beast of the night. A creature that comes out when the moon is full."

For a moment Jeff was stunned. He didn't know how to answer that. Logic told him that what Miguel had just said wasn't possible, but when he looked at the faces of all the men around him, he saw that they were serious and they truly believed this fairy tale. For a moment there was silence. No one said anything. Finally, Jeff broke the silence.

"That's the most ridiculous thing that I've ever heard."

"Still Señor, it is true. You will find that out. In time you will know the truth."

There was another long pause before Miguel spoke again.

"What are you going to do now, Señor?"

"Do now? Well, I'm going to take a nice long nap, then leave this crazy town with all the talk of beast-creatures and I'm going back to New York City."

Miguel nodded. "Yes, Señor, you are going to leave this town, but you will not leave the beast behind. No, you will take it with you. You will take it with you because the beast is hidden inside of you. It is part of you and it will stay there until the next full moon, then it will awaken and take over your body. Now you do not believe, but it will happen; then you will come to know. Then you will believe."

Jeff smiled, shook his head in disbelief and let out a little chuckle.

"You do not believe me, Señor. You think that we are all simple people who do not know the ways of the big world. That may be so, but one thing we do know, we know about these creatures. You may laugh at us, but when the full moon rises you will come to see that we are right and you will not laugh. But you will see signs before that. When the night of the full moon approaches you will feel the instincts and desires of a beast. You watch when you pee, you will see that your piss is no longer yellow but has turned to purple. When you see that, then you will know that what we say will soon happen."

Jeff looked at Miguel. All of this sounded so absurd to him. He wanted to say something to dismiss these dire warnings, these portents of doom. He wanted to laugh them off, but when he looked into the faces of Miguel and the men surrounding him, Jeff could see that they truly believed in the drivel that Miguel was spouting. Maybe these tales were just a type of native superstition, but when Jeff looked at the faces of the men around him, he saw a grave seriousness in their expressions. He saw that these people agreed with all that Miguel had said and that unnerved him.

Presently Jeff went back to his hotel. He walked through the front door up to the small desk and asked the clerk for his room key. He went up to his room where he pulled off his clothes and jumped into the shower.

The pulsing water felt good, so very good. It washed off all the dirt, grime, and sweat; it cleansed his entire body and at the same time refreshed his spirit. After a few minutes under the steady stream of water, Jeff got out of the shower, dried himself off and with only a towel wrapped around his waist, he fell onto the bed.

The mattress was a little stiff, but it was a pleasant change from the previous night spent on stones in a stream. He lay there, drifting off to a heavy sleep. The day after tomorrow, he would start back to New York City and when he returned home, everything would go back to normal—at least that's what he believed at the time. He had no idea how wrong he was.

The next day, Jeff packed his bag, paid his hotel bill and made his way back to Cozumel. From there he took a plane back to New York City. He was leaving Cozumel, the Yucatan jungles and the creatures of the night behind him. What he didn't realize was that as he left Cozumel and the Yucatan, the creature of the night would not be far behind.

CHAPTER 9

Jeff was back in the big city, the civilized world where science, fact and empirical evidence reigned. Now that he was on familiar turf, sitting before his word processor generating sleazy Cudmore copy, he felt like his old self again. He was now convinced that all which happened back in the jungles of Yucatan was just a figment of his imaginative past. The intensity of that moment on the moonlit mountain faded, somewhat like the emotion generated during a dramatic play dissipates when the curtain comes down and the house lights come up.

Now with all the modern amenities of city life, he was back to his old self. Everything was fine during the first week of his return.

During the second week, however, he began to notice miniscule differences in his being. He felt subtle changes in his body. At first these were slight alterations, nuances of emotion and behavior that made him feel and act slightly different, but they became more frequent as the days passed moving toward the full moon.

The first thing he noticed was that he was more sensitive to noise and sudden movements. Sometimes, the slightest rustle placed him on edge. Then he became aware of smells and odors around him, and he often found himself sniffing the air to sample the fragrances carried in the atmosphere. His sensitivity increased and he noticed that when the breeze was right, he could pick up smells and sensations from far away in the ether. The awareness of all the sights and sounds and smells around him were amplified and feeding directly into his enhanced sense receptors.

With each passing day, he felt this unexpected awareness making him increasingly restless and ever more agitated.

Soon there were other changes. One morning when he looked at his face in the mirror and noticed that there was new growth of hair between his eyebrows over the bridge of his nose. Funny, but it wasn't there the day before. This too was a minor thing. When he shaved, he simply used his razor to remove the unwanted hair. But the next morning it was back again, a whole new growth added that ran across the bridge of his nose and connected his eyebrows. Jeff thought it very strange that the hair grew so quickly. He'd never known of a male that grew hair so quickly. Now all this was happening about a week before the night of the full moon but Jeff still didn't make the connection.

The strangest thing, however, came two days before the full moon when he went into the men's room to relieve himself. As he was urinating, he stood looking at the wall before him with his mind lost in thought somewhere. But when he was finished and was zipping up his fly, he chanced to look down into the base of the urinal at the liquid that had collected there.

That's when he noticed the purple color. He was shocked to see that his urine had turned purple and at that moment he realized that something was very wrong. He recalled the warning that Miguel had sounded back in the Yucatan: *you will see that your piss is no longer yellow but has turned purple. When you see that, then you will know.* An icy chill seized Jeff as he realized that the dire prophecy that the natives of the Yucatan had warned him about might be coming true. Could he be slowly turning into a beast of the night?

Yet, contrary to all the mounting physical evidence, his rational mind could not accept the fact that a living, breathing, civilized man could turn into an animal. Surely that was just an old legend, a superstition and nothing more. Science had completely dispelled the werewolf legend and modern science illuminated truth and rejected falsehood.

The changes in his body, however, were telling him otherwise, and it didn't look good. Yet in spite of the many signs that his body was demonstrating, Jeff still tried to ignore it all. He tried to overlook the mounting evidence and to put it out of his mind by telling himself that these changes were only a temporary abnormality, perhaps caused by overwork and stress. He told himself that in time and with a little more rest, these physical aberrations would disappear and his body would return to normal. He tried hard to convince himself of that, but deep down his mind was engaged in a civil war.

On the eve of the full moon Jeff went home early because he felt a little peculiar—more so than usual—and just to be on the safe side, he decided that he should spend the night alone in his apartment where he could take it easy and turn in early.

He went back to his apartment, entered and locked and bolted his front door. Then he made himself a modest supper and had a few glasses of wine. For a time, all seemed to be going well and everything seemed normal. The wine took its effect and he fell asleep on the couch before the television.

Then as the night progressed, the full moon rose in the sky and its mysterious powers reached down to the sleeping adman. Jeff awoke with a sudden start because he felt all sorts of strange pains and aches coursing through his body. He knew that he was having some sort of attack and he knew that he desperately needed to call for help. He rolled off the couch and started to crawl toward the phone across the room. He never made it.

The attacks increased in intensity. He rolled over on his back and writhed in agony as the pains of the metamorphosis took hold. His body sprouted a dense, pelt of coarse hair. His hands and feet grew claws. His ears became long, hairy and pointed. His nose turned into a long protruding snout and his teeth elongated into sharp fangs. In less than ten minutes the aberrations were complete. Jefferson Foxlove had turned from a mild-mannered, civilized human being into a savage werewolf. With this change came a voracious appetite for living flesh, and a thirst for warm pumping blood.

Now in full wolf form, he went into his bedroom, opened the window and climbed out onto the fire escape. In a low crouch on padded paws he made his way down the metal stairs, then dropped into the alley. In the alley, on the ground level, he looked around and sniffed the air, ever wary that some adversary might be lurking nearby, but there was no one. It was after midnight and the streets were deserted.

Cautiously the werewolf crept to the end of the alley, and at the corner, he paused to look around for victims. He began prowling through the streets and back alleys, always keeping to the shadows, staying close to the walls and doorways, constantly sniffing the air for the scent of living prey. Undaunted, the wolf-creature continued on the prowl, intent on finding fresh meat. Finally, he came to the edge of the park, and there his acute sense of smell captured the scent of warm, living human flesh.

He entered the park. There was some sort of prey nearby—human or animal. Effortlessly he moved through the bushes following the scent that drifted in the air. At last his search was rewarded; he came to a deserted corner of the park with a solitary bench on which sat two young lovers entwined in a passionate embrace under the light of the full moon.

Cautiously, the beast dropped to all fours and crept closer. With stealth and cunning born of innate animal instinct, the werewolf silently approached his unsuspecting victims. The man and woman were in rapture enjoying an amorous moment. They had no idea that death was so close and that the end of their lives could conceivably be only seconds away.

The wolfman moved even closer and crouched in the nearby bushes. There was a pause as he studied his victims, while at the same time, he tensed all of his muscles, and gathered his strength as he planned the exact moment for his strike. Finally, when he was confident that the auspicious moment had arrived, he sprang from the bushes and attacked.

The woman let out a scream at the sight of the hideous creature who had suddenly appeared from nowhere. Petrified, she froze in place. The man turned and tried to offer some defense, but he was caught off guard and besides, his puny strength was no match for the superior power of the werewolf. The beast killed the man, then went for the woman. In a manner of minutes, it was all over. The werewolf had found two victims, killed them and had satiated himself with their flesh and their blood. His conquest was complete, his appetite rewarded. He raised his snout to the moonlit sky and howled. Thus, the creature of the night, spawned in the jungles of the Yucatan had found new territory in New York City.

CHAPTER 10

The next morning Jeff woke up on the sofa with the television still blaring. He rolled over and sat up on the edge of the couch and put his hands to his head. He was still groggy from his deep sleep–slow to grasp his bearings. As he sat there bringing his mind into focus, he considered his circumstance. It seemed to him as if he'd dozed that evening on the couch in front of the television, and had dropped off into a deep, sound sleep. But it was a sleep plagued with a horrible nightmare of killing and carnage.

This nightmare was troubling because it seemed so vivid and graphic that it seemed almost real. It was like that terrible dream he had a month ago on top of the mountain in the Yucatan. But this time he could not attribute it to the food. He wondered why he was having such terrible, graphic, nocturnal visions. What had he done to bring them about?

This was a question that he would consider later. For now, he just shook his head violently to purge the remnants of sleep from his brain. He told himself that what he had was simply a nightmare, a figment of fantasy, conjured up by a creative brain. There was no substance to it. It didn't really happen.

It couldn't have been real because nothing had changed. He went to sleep on the couch in his apartment with the television on and he awoke the very next morning on the same couch in front of the television. Everything was exactly the same as when he fell asleep. No ripped-up clothing, no blood, no victim, no complaints from the people next door; it was all an imagination gone wild.

He rose from the couch, went into the bathroom and ran cold water into the lavatory. He was about to scoop up the water and splash it on his face, but when he reached out, he saw his hands. He saw that his fingers were caked with dried blood. He looked into the mirror. That's when he saw the dried blood around his mouth and on his shirt and pants. Jeff raised his head and cried out in fear and anguish. Something very real had happened.

Jeff sank down onto the toilet seat. Sometime during the night, he had actually changed into the unthinkable and gone on the prowl. He had become a savage, ruthless creature that went out stalking for prey and found two victims. He attacked and killed them. During the night, he'd turned into a killer beast, a werewolf.

He remained on the toilet seat trying to decide what to do. After much consideration, Jeff decided that he had to go to the police and turn himself in. Of course, he assumed the authorities wouldn't believe his tale of becoming a werewolf, but he knew if he showed them his blood-stained clothes they would have to take notice. They would believe him when they examined his evidence.

So, Jeff shaved and showered and dressed, and with the bag of bloody clothes in hand, he left his apartment and headed for the nearest police station. He'd walked only one block when he stopped to think. He realized that he would probably be with the police for some time, and he might not have the opportunity to let anyone know what happened or where he was. Jeff considered that and decided that maybe before going to the police he should drop by the office and let Mr. Cudmore know what happened and what he was going to do. That seemed like the reasonable thing to do so with that intent, Jeff turned and headed for Madison Avenue.

When Jeff got to the office he went directly to Damon Cudmore's office. The door was open. Cudmore was sitting at his desk reading the newspaper with a bagel and coffee. Jeff knocked on the door frame and announced that he had an urgent matter to discuss, and it was something that couldn't wait. Naturally, Cudmore was surprised and curious by the gravity and insistence in the young man's manner. It was obvious that Jeff was agitated about something, so Cudmore waved for him to take a seat.

Jeff lost no time in coming to the point.

"Mr. Cudmore, I'm sorry but I'm going to have to leave the agency."

Damon Cudmore blanched at those words. He didn't like what he was hearing. The thought of losing his best copywriter, his dedicated disciple, the boy that he'd hand-picked and trained, caused Cudmore's blood pressure to rise, yet he maintained his outward composure, minimizing any reaction until he found out exactly what was bothering his young protégé. He looked warily at Jeff.

"Why are you saying this, Jeff? Have you gotten a better offer from some other agency? Because if you have, I'll—"

"No, it's nothing like that."

"Are you tired of the ad game?"

"No, not that either."

"Well, what? What's got you in such a dither anyway?"

"Last night I committed a horrible crime and I know that I must go to the police and give myself up."

Cudmore stared at Jeff in amazement. "For heaven's sake why? What have you done?"

"Mr. Cudmore, last night I killed two people."

"What? What the hell do you mean? Do you have any idea what it is you're saying?"

"Yes sir, I do."

"You're telling me that you are a murderer."

"Well, not me exactly. That is to say that it was me that did the killing, but it wasn't me in this form, so it was me but not me as I am now. It was sort of another me."

Cudmore shook his head in disbelief. "What the hell are you talking about? Come on, man, do I need to call the men in the white coats?"

"Mr. Cudmore, I've become a werewolf. Last night during the full moon, I changed into my other form, and as a wolfman I went out and killed two people."

Cudmore looked back at Jeff in wide-eyed amazement; for a moment he wasn't exactly sure that he heard the young man correctly.

Finally, he spoke up. "Ah come on, Jeff, you ought to know better than to con the master conman. Too much late-night television, too many weird movies. Maybe you're on something, like some sort of recreational drug, but you've taken leave of your senses and—"

"No, it's true Mr. Cudmore. I'm not imagining things. Look, I can prove it."

With that Jeff reached down and picked up the plastic bag that was beside his feet. He reached into it and pulled out a shirt and a pair of pants. They were covered in fresh, dried blood.

"You see these are the clothes that I wore last night. You see the blood. This isn't my blood. It's the blood of the victims, the people I killed. You see it's true. Last night I turned into a werewolf and went on the prowl."

Cudmore looked down at the clothes and back into Jeff's face. For a moment he didn't say anything, but Jeff could see that the wheels of thought turning in the big man's mind.

After a long pause, Cudmore asked, "These people you say you killed; were any of them our clients?"

"No," said Jeff, "but they—"

"Okay, then it's not serious. Look Jeff, trust me, you don't want to go to the authorities with this tale. All right? Trust me on this."

"But Mr. Cudmore, don't you realize that last night I killed two human beings."

"But Jeff, this is the big city. Killings are happening all the time. There are over eight million people in this place. A couple more or less won't make any difference. I tell you it's nothing to get alarmed about."

"But I'm a werewolf now. I really am. This will happen again. This will happen to me every month when the full moon rises."

Now Damon Cudmore didn't know whether to believe this werewolf story or not; maybe it was just some sort of delusion on Jeff's part, a bad dream. That seemed plausible, but then he looked back at the bloodied clothes, and wondered whether there was a kernel of truth somewhere in Jeff's bizarre tale. Obviously, something had happened, and maybe it was violent. Still Cudmore knew that he couldn't let Jeff go to the police because they would most likely lock the boy up for life and Cudmore didn't want to lose his best copywriter.

"All right, so what's one little killing here and there? You can't quit the ad game just because of that."

Jeff moaned aloud. He was so distraught. This was serious, tragic business, but somehow, he couldn't seem to make Cudmore realize the gravity of it.

"Mr. Cudmore, you don't seem to understand; I'm a murderer."

"No, you're not, Jeff. You're not a murderer because you didn't kill those people as you. You did it in the world's most grisly nightmare, or at worst in another form."

At this point Cudmore wasn't sure whether he really believed this werewolf story or not, but he decided to take another tack and launch a counter argument.

"If what you say is true—and I'm not saying that it is, mind you, but if it is, then you did it as an animal, not as a man. That demonstrates the killing part of the natural order of life. You can't be blamed for that."

"But sir—" Jeff protested. Cudmore cut him off.

"Look Jeff, this is classic survival of the fittest. Lions kill zebras all the time. Nobody puts them in jail."

"But Mr. Cudmore, we're talking about human beings here, not lions in the jungle. I killed two innocent people last night and I have to be put away."

Cudmore pursed his lips. His argument wasn't going as smoothly as he'd hoped, but undaunted, he continued,

"Jeff, look at it this way. Every year hundreds of thousands of people die in automobile accidents and human error. They get bumped off and they're dead, but no one talks about scrapping the automobile."

"But Mr. Cudmore, with all due respect, I don't think that's the same thing."

"Don't think, Jeff. It'll only get you into trouble. Let me do the thinking for the both of us. That's what I'm good at."

Cudmore could see that his young protégé was confused but at the same time he sensed that the young man was starting to weaken, so he pressed forward with another argument.

"Now Jeff, look at it this way. It's like when a woman has her period every month; she becomes bitchy and cranky, but no one blames her for that because it's a part of a natural cycle."

"But women don't kill people when they are having their periods."

"Some of them do. It's been known to happen; and when they do, they say it was PMS that drove them to murder. The courts always let them off because it's an act of nature."

"But Mr. Cudmore," cried a distraught Jeff, "I have to be locked up or else I'll kill again. The next time the full moon comes out, I'll become a wolf and go out and kill again. I have to be put in jail. I don't want to kill any more innocent people."

"No, Jeff, you don't have to be put in jail. And you won't kill again. I promise you that. Believe me, I'll see that you don't."

"But how can you prevent it? I mean, when the moon rises and—"

"Now don't you worry. I said I'll take care of it, and I will. I'll find a way. For now, you just go back to your office and write some copy that'll grab the consumer by the short hairs. Let me worry about what happened last night. Don't give this matter a second thought; I assure you that I'll be on top of the whole situation."

"But I really think that I should go to the authorities and —"

"Now, I told you not to think. Let me do that, and let's have no more talk about going to the authorities. I told you, I'll take care of everything and believe me, I will. Now be a good boy and get back to your word processor. Leave this bag of clothes here. If you take them with you, they'll only distract you.

Come on, Jeff, let's have no more arguments. I told you I'd think of something and I will. You just go back to your keyboard and start writing some dynamite copy."

Reluctantly, Jeff dragged himself back to his cubicle.

After Jeff left the office, Damon Cudmore walked to his door, poked his head out into the corridor and shouted, "Willard, get your ass into my office!"

Immediately upon hearing his name called out, Willard Plotkin came running. Willard Plotkin was an earnest young man who was rather small in stature. He had very large ears, a small nose and an unruly mop of close cropped sandy brown hair

Standing at only five foot two inches tall, Willard Plotkin looked more like a large mouse than a human being, and he had a temperament to match. He never said very much because he had a meek, introverted personality. He always preferred to answer questions and respond to comments rather than initiate any kind of statement.

Willard was the office gofer, and as such, he was always at Cudmore's beck and call. At least two or three times a day, Damon Cudmore would poke his head out of his office and shout, "Willard, get your ass into my office!" and no matter where he was Willard would always come running to answer his master's call.

This time when he heard the call, he was on the other side of the office bay, but in a flash, he ran through the corridors to Cudmore's office and presented himself to the big kiwi himself.

"Yes Mr. Cudmore, you called me?"

"Yes, I did Willard. I want you to do something for me. I want you to keep an eye on Jeff Foxlove. He's taken it into his head that he has committed a crime. Of course, there's no basis for this crazy idea, but he thinks there is. Now what I want you to do is watch him. If it looks like he's going out of the office for any reason, I want you to stop him until I get there. I don't want him going to the police. You got that?"

"Well, I'm not sure, sir. What exactly did Jeff think he did that would make him want to go to the police?"

"Willard, don't ask questions. You're not paid to ask questions, only to follow orders. You got that?"

"Yes sir, Mr. Cudmore."

"Okay then, you watch Foxlove and if he does anything suspicious, then you call me."

"Yes sir."

"Good! Now you get your ass in gear and keep an eye on Foxlove. And remember, I'm counting on you!"

Willard went and did as he was told.

With Willard keeping watch over Jeff Foxlove, Cudmore felt that he could devote his energies to the problem at hand. He retreated back into his office, sat down in his chair and leaned back, thinking about all that Jeff had just told him. This was a dilemma to be reckoned with, but Cudmore was sure he could come up with a workable solution; all he had to do was apply his genius.

He realized that his protégé, Jeff Foxlove whom he'd nurtured to be the best copywriter he'd in years, had the desire to turn himself into the authorities just because he actually believed he was a werewolf. Of course, the whole idea was preposterous. But then Cudmore looked down at the bag with the bloody clothes that Jeff had brought in.

Yes, those clothes were possible evidence that Jeff did go out and kill a few people. But so what? After all, what are a couple of murders here and there? Those things were happening every day in New York City. As far as Cudmore was concerned, two murders of nameless insignificant people were certainly no big deal. What truly bothered Cudmore was the fact that the boy had suddenly developed a conscience. Didn't he know that good advertising men put no stock in such old outdated ideas?

And now it seemed that the young man was set on turning himself in to the authorities. If he did that, then the police would lock him up, and he would be lost to the advertising world, especially to the world of Damon Cudmore. Cudmore just couldn't face the prospect of losing his prize disciple. This certainly was a quandary, but he was sure there was a workable solution…somewhere. He thought about it for a long time; then he had a sudden inspiration. He reached for the phone book, looked up a number and called the Brooklyn Iron and Steel Works.

CHAPTER 11

Well, for the next couple of weeks things were more or less the same at the Cudmore Agency. Jeff did as Damon Cudmore told him; he came to the office every day, worked at his job, and did not go to the police. He continued to write copy and create ads, and for a short time, all was well with him. But then as the days and nights went by and the night of the full moon drew near, Jeff became increasingly anxious. He could feel the incremental changes shaping his body and soul and he knew that soon he would be at the mercy of the evil forces of nature and would turn into a ravenous, predatory beast again.

From time to time, Jeff expressed his anxiety to his boss, but Cudmore nonchalantly replied that he had the matter well in hand and told Jeff not to worry. Well, that was easier said than done, because as far as Jeff could see, Cudmore hadn't done anything to change the situation. Jeff continued to bide his time, trusting that his boss had some solution in the works. Yet as the night of the full moon drew closer, Cudmore still hadn't revealed any plan and Jeff became increasingly anxious.

Finally, the fateful day came. At the end of that day, when the sun went down and dusk took over. Very soon the full moon would rise and create the terrible metamorphosis that Jeff feared. At five o'clock, quitting time, Jeff marched into Damon Cudmore's office.

"Mr. Cudmore, I can't wait any longer. Soon the full moon will be up and I'll become a werewolf and go out and attack someone. I can't let that happen. I must go to the police."

Cudmore looked up from his desk with a slight smile on his face.

"Now hold on, Jeff! I told you that I'd take care of everything, and I have. Come on, I'll show you what I've worked out."

Cudmore rose from behind his desk, walked over and put his arm around Jeff's shoulder in a paternal gesture.

"Come on, I've got something to show you in the sub-basement."

He led Jeff from the office and the two men started down the corridor toward the freight elevator. At the elevator door, Cudmore paused.

"Maybe we should get Willard to join us. He might be useful." Cudmore turned and shouted, "Willard, get your ass over here!"

In less than a minute Willard appeared before Cudmore and Jeff.

"You called me, Mr. Cudmore?"

"Yeah Willard, I did. Jeff and I are going down to the sub-basement. I want to show him something and I think you should come along too."

Willard nodded even though he was wary. Cudmore always said his job was not to reason why but to duly comply. The three men got into the freight elevator and rode it all the way down to the sub-basement. When the car stopped and the doors opened, Cudmore led the way to a dark corner of a remote section of the sub-basement. He flipped on the wall switch and illuminated a large object against the wall; then he proudly turned to Jeff and Willard.

"Well?" he asked.

Jeff walked forward and looked at the object.

"It's a cage!"

"That's right!" Cudmore grinned. "I had the Brooklyn Iron and Steel Works come over and put it together for me. The whole thing is made of high-quality steel. The bars, the floor, the top, the hinges, all steel. This baby is super strong. Everything is welded together. It will hold even the most powerful werewolf."

"You intend to put me in a cage?"

"Only for the night, Jeffy Boy. And maybe for the next night…only as long as the full moon supposedly turns you into a wolf. Then in the morning when you change back again, I'll let you out and you can resume being your old self again."

Jeff looked at the cage skeptically. "Gee, Mr. Cudmore, I don't know if this is a good idea."

"Of course it is, Jeffy Boy. Think of it this way; if you went to the police, they'd lock you up. Only they'd throw away the key and keep you in jail for the rest of your life. You'd never get out again. This way, we lock up at night and let you out in the morning; and we only have to do that a couple of nights each month. I tell you it's better this way. Now be a good fellow and get in the cage."

With some reluctance Jeff got into the cage. Cudmore closed the door and fastened the padlock. He put the key in his pocket then walked over to a nearby stool and sat down.

"Now we wait," he announced.

Willard went over to Cudmore and asked in a low voice, "I don't get it, Mr. Cudmore. Why are we putting Jeff into a cage?"

"He's got some crazy idea that he's going to turn into a werewolf. I think it's a lot of nonsense, but I thought I'd humor him. Anyway, let's wait and see what happens."

At the end of two hours nothing had occurred. Jeff remained locked up in the cage. Cudmore and Willard sat outside watching and waiting for something, but…nothing. Another hour passed. Cudmore remained seated on a stool filing his fingernails, occasionally looking over to see if Jeff was becoming more feral, more beast-like, but no, he was still human; only now he was lying fast asleep on the floor of the cage.

Willard edged over to Cudmore.

"Mr. Cudmore, sir, it doesn't look like anything is happening. I don't think Jeff is really going to turn into a werewolf."

"Don't think, Willard. You're not getting paid to think. Jeff told me that the whole thing happens during the full moon. Maybe the moon's not up yet. Let's wait a bit more before we give up on this."

Willard nodded and went back to the empty crate he was sitting on. Fifteen more minutes passed and still there was no change. Just when it looked like the whole experiment would come to nothing, Jeff let out a low grunt. Cudmore looked up; his eyes narrowed and he stared intently at the sleeping figure in the cage. Willard leaned forward.

Jeff moaned and then started thrashing about. He moaned again and again, then his moans turned into growls. The cage was dimly lit by one meager overhead light, and Jeff was thrashing about so wildly, it was difficult to tell exactly what was happening to him; but it was obvious that he was in the throes of some sort of seizure. There was more growling and snarling as the lone figure in the cage rolled around in apparent agony.

Willard looked anxiously back at Damon Cudmore.

"Shouldn't we call a doctor or the paramedics or something?"

Cudmore shook his head. "No, Willard. Jeff said something like this would happen, and if he's really becoming a werewolf, then no doctor can help. Let's just wait this out."

They didn't have long to wait. In less than five minutes, Jeff Foxlove was no more; in his place stood a vicious, snarling, hairy beast of a werewolf. The newly-transformed creature jumped around in the cage, rattled the bars and tried to break free of its constraints but the steel held firm. The creature of the night was locked up and he could not get out.

Willard looked on in horror at the beast that Jeff Foxlove had become. He looked back at Cudmore.

"Sir," he said, "this is horrible. It's simply terrible."

Cudmore had been watching the whole transformation with interest and when the conversion was complete and the werewolf in the cage stared out with angry eyes and drooling fangs, Cudmore stroked his chin and simply said, "Well, I'll be damned."

"Oh Mr. Cudmore," cried Willard. "We have to do something."

A slight smile formed on Damon Cudmore's lips. "Yes Willard. You're right, and we will do something."

Now all this time Cudmore had been watching the same scene as Willard. He saw the same vicious werewolf, pulling at the bars, foaming at the mouth, but at the same time a different picture was forming in his brain. He was seeing possibilities that had escaped the diminutive, little Willard.

Little Willard placed a trembling hand over his eyes.

"Oh, this is horrible," he said.

"Maybe this is horrible, Willard, and then again, maybe not," he murmured cryptically.

"But Mr. Cudmore, think of what poor Jeff must be going through."

"Indeed Willard, it must be a strain on Jeff, but in a couple of days he'll be back to normal again and he'll be all right. In the meantime, remember that behind every dark cloud there is a silver lining; and keep in mind that in the world of advertising there is always a way to turn that silver lining into profit."

Willard looked up at Cudmore, wondering what the big man was alluding to. He waited for some explanation but Cudmore said nothing more. Yet Willard could see that his boss was thinking, planning, plotting, scheming. As Cudmore stood there looking at the snarling, hairy werewolf rattling the bars of the cage, the wheels in his devious mind were turning. Willard had no way of knowing, but Damon Cudmore was silently concocting another one of his convoluted schemes.

And the more Cudmore thought about his latest brainstorm, the more he believed that the light of inspiration was shining on him, and he smiled in satisfaction as he thought about the possibilities that lay ahead.

CHAPTER 12

After the full moon faded there was no need for Jeff to be caged up, well at least not until the next month. In the interim he could be free to continue with his normal routine. Thus, it seemed that after his first experience in the sub-basement, Jeff was more or less back on track with his life. Of course, his life wasn't exactly the same as it was before he took his vacation in the Yucatan, but it was as close to normalcy as he could get.

All things considered, Jeff felt that he could make the adjustment to this new lifestyle mode because, well, after all, there was nothing else he could do to change his bizarre nature. So, he was more or less content to continue this way, knowing that as long as he was locked up during the periods of the full moon, then his violence would be contained. He would still change into a werewolf, but at least he wouldn't be running everywhere feasting on innocent people's blood. The best he could do, under the circumstances, was to accept the situation and make the best of it.

Jeff therefore assumed that everything would be the same the following month during the full moon. What Jeff Foxlove did not know, however, was that Damon Cudmore saw a hidden opportunity in Jeff's werewolf being and he started to take advantage of his next full-moon transformation. When the next month rolled around, on the night of the full moon, Jeff dutifully stepped into the cage. He was totally unaware that Cudmore had two men covertly waiting in another part of the sub-basement. They remained out of sight until Jeff was safely locked in the steel enclosure. As soon as he saw that Jeff was fast asleep on the floor of the cage, Cudmore gave the signal and the two men emerged from the shadows.

"Okay boys," he said, "you can set up your equipment right here. Don't get too close to the cage. Not yet, not until we find out how wild he's gonna be. We can move in for a close-up later on."

The two men nodded in silent agreement and started their set-up. One man set up the lights, the other pulled a tripod out of a packing case and positioned a camera on it. When everything was in position they gave Cudmore the high sign and stood by awaiting further instructions.

Willard, who was also standing by, looked up at his boss.

"Sir, why are these men here? And what are they going to do?"

"What do they look like, Willard? They're my camera crew, and they're gonna take pictures."

"Oh, Mr. Cudmore!" said Willard. "Don't tell me you're going to take pictures of Jeff as he turns into a werewolf."

"No, of course not! What do I look like? Some sort of circus hack who runs a freak show? Give me some credit, boy. I've got bigger fish to fry, something grander in mind."

"I don't understand, sir, exactly what are you planning to do?"

"No more questions, Willard. You're not getting paid to ask questions. Just wait and see. Very soon everything will be revealed."

So Cudmore, Willard, the cameraman, and the lighting technician stood before the cage waiting for the full moon to rise and the young man behind the bars to transform himself from man to beast. Everyone was silent as they waited for the change to happen. It wasn't long before the metamorphosis began and in a very short time—less than five minutes— the four men were staring at a caged wolf-man.

The beast arose from the floor of the cage stood upright, and looked out. At first nothing happened. The five figures, the wolf-man in the cage and the four men outside, just stood there waiting and watching and looking at each other. Then suddenly the wolf-man came to life. He snarled, bared his fangs, and leaped forward to attack the spectators but was stopped by the steel bars. He extended his arms through the bars, waving them, trying to tear at anything and everything that he could sink his claws into. Everything, however, was beyond his reach. He growled, snarled, pulled at the bars and rattled the cage. The steel held and the wolf-man remained firmly confined, powerless to break out.

Damon Cudmore smiled at the beast's frustration and he figured that now was the time to put his plan into action. He reached down to a package that lay on the table beside him. He ripped the paper open and pulled out two slabs of raw meat, then he stepped forward and held up a piece of meat in each hand.

The wolfman snarled and reached out to grab Cudmore and the raw meat, but Cudmore remained safely out of reach.

He spoke in a soft, soothing voice. "Hey, Jeffy boy, calm down. It's me, your friendly, caring boss. Come on son, you know me. I'm the guy who always looks out for you. I'm the one who's always in your corner, always caring for you. You know me, don't you?"

At the sound of Cudmore's voice, the wolf-man calmed down a little. He lowered his limbs and stared back at the figure standing in front of him with two slabs of meat in each hand. It was obvious from the expression on his face that the wolf-man was puzzled and was trying to figure out what that weirdo with the meat was doing, and what he was leading up to. The wolf-man just stood there, waiting and watching; he didn't have to wait long to find out what was coming.

Cudmore continued. "Now look, Jeffy boy, I've got this lovely, delicious raw meat. Just look how big these steaks are. And they're fresh and raw, and dripping with yummy blood. You know you want them."

Cudmore slowly waved the two big steaks about in circles before the caged beast, tantalizing him with their goodness. The wolf-man looked back at two orbiting slabs of meat and followed them with his eyes. He smelled their essence, and his mouth drooled as he imagined their juicy goodness, but he couldn't get at them because Cudmore held them beyond his grasp.

"Now Jeffy boy, I'm gonna give you this delicious meat—I really am—but first I want you to do something for me. Okay?"

The wolf-man said nothing, not one growl or snarl, but Cudmore seemed to detect a light of recognition, a glimmer of agreement in his eyes. He stepped back and turned to his cameraman.

"I think he's gonna go for this. Max turn on the lights. Gus, start your camera. I want you to get every bit of this on film."

The lights came on. Under the glare of the lights the wolfman stepped back. The cameraman flipped a switch on his camera and a steady purr sounded from within the instrument.

"Okay, we're rolling boss."

"Good," said Cudmore as he put the steaks down on the table. Then he reached into a small bag and pulled out a can of shaving cream and he approached the cage again, slowly and deliberately; but he remained cautious, ready to jump away if the wolf-man suddenly became violent.

The beast, however, remained calm, possibly because the bright lights unnerved him and because he was still bewildered by what was going on.

When Cudmore was within arm's length, he gingerly extended his arm to hand over the can of shaving cream.

"Come on Jeffy boy, take this. It won't hurt you. It's a can of Beardblob shaving cream. You know Beardblob, don't you? Sure you do, that's one of our clients. Come on, Jeffy boy, take the can."

At first the wolf-man was hesitant, but with Cudmore's smooth, coaxing voice he came forward, reached out and accepted the can of shaving cream. Cudmore stepped back again.

"Good!" said Cudmore. "Now, Jeffy boy I want you to move back, to the rear of the cage away from these bars."

The beast slowly backed away.

"Ah, that's a good wolfman."

Cudmore turned to his camera man.

"Gus, move in tight. Get the lens between the bars. I don't want any of the cage to show in the frame."

Gus nodded and moved forward.

"In position, boss. No bars in the frame."

"Good," said Cudmore. "Now Jeffy boy, I want you to start spreading the cream over your hairy face, just around the mouth, your cheeks, and under your chin."

Again, the wolf-man was hesitant as if he were trying to understand what was happening and why he was in this strange situation. Cudmore continued to coax in his soothing voice.

"Come on, you can do it. Do it for me, Jeffy. Do this for your old boss, the guy who always looks out for you. Do this for me. Do this for me and I'll give you some nice, juicy, raw meat."

Slowly but surely, the beast started to do as Cudmore directed. He squirted a dollop of shaving cream into his paw and started to spread it around the lower half of his face, around his mouth and under his chin.

Cudmore turned to the lighting technician. "Make sure you keep the light on him. I don't want any shadows on his face. We won't get a retake if anything goes wrong."

"I'm watching, boss. Don't worry, the lighting will be perfect. Nothing'll go wrong."

Cudmore reached into his little bag and pulled out a razor. He stepped up to the cage again and handed the razor to the beast within. With some hesitation the werewolf took the razor and looked curiously at it. Cudmore, ever cautious, stepped back to a safe distance should the wolfman suddenly become violent again.

"Now Jeffy boy, I want you to take the razor and start shaving your face. That's it, just take the razor and shave away all that nasty, ugly hair. And when you do, I'll give you the meat. Go ahead, Jeffy, just shave your face. You'll feel better after you do."

The wolf-man, still a little hesitant, started to do as Cudmore asked. He put the razor up to his cheek, under one hairy, pointed ear and dragged it down. The hair was cut away, revealing clean flesh underneath.

Gus, the cameraman, looked up from the eyepiece at Cudmore.

"I think he's going for it. It looks like he's gonna do it."

Cudmore smiled a wry, calculated smile. "Yeah! He's gonna do it all right. Watch closely boys, we're gonna make advertising history with this one."

Cudmore turned his attention back to the cage and continued to direct the wolf-man through the entire shaving sequence until at last, the beast was clean shaven. Well, at least his lower face was hairless. The rest of the beast remained covered with dense coarse hair and he still had hairy, pointed ears. That presented a strange and curious sight, for here was a hairy beast with a clean-shaven chin while the rest of his face and ears was covered with dense, coarse animal hair.

When it was all over, Cudmore ordered the camera stopped and the lights turned off. He threw the slabs of meat into the cage and turned to his accomplices.

"Well, boys, we did it. I think we just filmed a commercial that will rock the advertising world. When this baby hits the airwaves, it'll knock everybody's socks off."

The cameraman and lighting technician nodded in recognition.

During this entire incident, while they were filming the shaving scene, Willard stood by, silently watching the entire sequence. At first, he wasn't sure what it was the Cudmore was trying to do or why he was doing it. It was only at the very end that Willard realized that Damon Cudmore was using the wolfman to make a shaving commercial.

When they were all finished, the camera crew packed up the equipment and departed. Cudmore and Willard continued to stand by and watch the ravenous werewolf devour the raw meat. Satisfied that all had gone according to plan, Cudmore flipped off the ceiling light and started walking for the elevator. Willard followed in his wake.

In the elevator Willard looked up at Cudmore and asked, "Mr. Cudmore, sir, are you really going to put that film on the airwaves?"

Cudmore replied with a broad, self-satisfied smile, "Damn right I am! Willard, m'boy, what you just witnessed was a sample of the Cudmore genius at work. When this commercial starts running, the whole advertising world will sit up and take notice!"

"Yes sir, I'm sure it will, but is it right to use Jeff in this way?"

"Willard, m'boy, we're not using Jeff!"

"We're not?"

"No. What we're doing is allowing another side of Jeff, his wolfman image to be displayed. No one will know that it is really Jeff Foxlove in the commercial, but this will allow Jeff's creative talent to come forth. All we're doing is providing the means for him to shine in the spotlight. That's what working in advertising is all about, finding your place in the spotlight."

Damon Cudmore was all smiles with that explanation, but Willard looked up at him with some skepticism.

CHAPTER 13

It wasn't long before the commercial of the wolfman shaving off his coarse facial hair was running on television. The ad captured the imagination of the consumer public and the sales of Beardblob shaving cream went through the roof. The client was a happy camper and Damon Cudmore was immensely pleased with himself.

In addition, his prophecy came true: the whole advertising world did sit up and take notice. The werewolf commercial had been so imaginative and so real that the creative brains in all the other agencies had to wonder exactly how Cudmore pulled it off. Of course, everyone believed that Cudmore had hired an actor and had some expert cosmetician apply that fantastic makeup, but still, the makeup looked so real and the actor was so true to life, that the final effect was uncanny in the extreme.

Secretly, other agencies hired actors and brought in make-up specialists and cosmetologists in an effort to create the same effect, but try as they might, they just couldn't do it. Some guys in the creative departments also experimented with computer animation in an attempt to produce their own monster images, but that didn't work either. Their results weren't as realistic as the Cudmore werewolf commercial. Cudmore had created a surprisingly realistic wolfman and everyone on Madison Avenue scratched their heads and wondered how he did it.

So, Damon Cudmore was on top of the world, strutting around his office like a proud peacock, puffed up with the feeling that he was the supreme creative genius of the advertising world and that he could do no wrong. It was as if the advertising world was now his oyster and nothing and nobody could stop him from reigning supreme as the impresario of Madison Avenue.

During all this speculation, Cudmore remained smug and confident. He knew that he had a gold mine of advertising campaigns with his own private werewolf and he knew that nobody else could copy his commercials. He was determined to ride the werewolf train for all it was worth. Indeed, at that time it looked like he could go on forever using his captive werewolf to generate all sorts of ads for hair products, tooth products, deodorants, and you name it.

However, what Cudmore—and indeed most of the others at the agency—didn't realize at the time was that something was happening to change everything. Damon Cudmore wasn't aware of it, but there was a tiny fissure in his glorious world that was about to widen and threaten all he had recently accomplished.

The first signs of this disintegration were very subtle. Something was happening to Jeff Foxlove. After that first shooting session for Beardblob, the full moon had passed and Jeff had shaken off his werewolf persona he returned to his human form and was, by all outward appearances, his old self—yet at the same time, he was different. Somehow, he wasn't as vibrant and energetic as before. He was a little less alert, a bit lethargic and a little more fatigued than usual.

Well, even the few people who noticed this subtle change attributed it to lack of sleep or maybe overwork and they dismissed his condition as something that was only temporary, something that would pass after Jeff got rest over the weekend. But then the weekend came and went, and when Jefferson Foxlove returned to the office, he wasn't any better.

When the next full moon came, Cudmore arranged another shooting session for his wolf man actor. This time the commercial was for a shampoo and conditioner. It showed the werewolf shampooing his unruly mane then rinsing and applying the conditioner, then combing his unruly mane into place. The result was a wolf man with a neatly styled coiffure.

After the film was edited and the appropriate voice-over dubbed in, Cudmore viewed the commercial on his big screen. He pronounced it to be a smashing success and he was elated. Confidence in his werewolf was still growing and he was definitely going to hit the jackpot with another brilliant werewolf campaign. Indeed, when it hit the airwaves, it was enthusiastically received by a receptive consumer audience and sales for the shampoo and conditioner rose to unprecedented levels. Once again, the big man was riding high, wide, and handsome in the advertising world.

His joy was short-lived, however, because two days later when Jeff came back to the office, once again after having returned to his human form, the changes that were so subtle before were now painfully evident. His movements were slow, tired, and weak; his face was drawn and there were pronounced dark circles under his eyes. His frame was thinner; he had lost considerable weight. Poor Jeff looked like he had been run over by a truck, and now it was evident to everyone that there was something drastically wrong with the young, werewolf-copywriter. Now even Cudmore noticed Jeff's pallid condition, and he knew that if he didn't do something soon he would lose his star performer.

Cudmore called Jeff into his office for a fatherly chat. He had Jeff sit down and he took up a chair next to him. Then he leaned over so he was close to Jeff. When he looked directly in his face, he didn't like what he saw. Jeff's face was pale and his skin looked kind of pasty. His eyes were dull and lackluster. Moreover, it looked to Cudmore as if something inside of Jeff, some vestige of spirit, was lost. It was obvious to Cudmore that the boy was seriously ill.

"Jeff, m'boy, you don't look so good, and frankly, I'm concerned. Tell me, how are you feeling?"

"Not so good, Mr. Cudmore. Lately I've felt tired and kind of weak."

"Yes, I can see that. Well, have you been getting enough sleep?"

"Yes, and then again no. I mean that I get to bed early each night, and I immediately drop off to sleep. I sleep through the whole night and get my eight hours of sleep, but somehow when I get up in the morning I don't feel at all rested. It's as if I don't really get a deep sleep. I don't know why but I just can't seem to get a sound sleep."

"Well, how about food? Are you eating enough? Are you getting your vitamins?"

"I take vitamins every day, but they don't seem to be helping at all. As for food, somehow all food seems to have lost its flavor and I don't feel like eating much."

"Hmmm. This sounds rather serious. I think that maybe you ought to see a doctor. I'll tell you what; I'm going to send you over to my personal physician. He'll find out what ails you and probably fix you up by giving you a shot of something or other. I'll get Willard to go with you, just to make sure you get there safely."

Cudmore got up from his chair, walked to the door, stuck his head out into the corridor and shouted, "Willard, get your ass in here!"

At the sound of his master's voice, Willard came running.

"Yes sir, Mr. Cudmore. You called me?"

"Damn right I did. Now listen Willard, I want you to take Jeff to my doctor. Here, I've written down the address on this card. Now you get Jeff to this address and stay there while the doctor is examining him. When he's finished, the two of you come back here. You got that?"

"Yes sir, I've got it."

"Good! As soon as you leave the office, I'll call the doc and tell him you're on the way and alert him as to the problem. Okay?"

"Yes sir, Mr. Cudmore."

"Good. So, latch on to Jeff there and get your ass in gear. Let me know when you get back. Oh, and Willard," said Cudmore in a hushed tone, "don't say anything to the doctor about Jeff being a werewolf. I don't think that's the kind of thing that should be broadcast around. Got that?"

Willard nodded.

Willard left the office with Jeff in tow. The two went uptown to Cudmore's personal physician. The doctor examined Jeff from head to toe but could find nothing wrong with him. He gave the young man a shot of vitamins but they didn't help, because after a week, Jeff was still the same. Stymied, the good doctor suggested that Jeff go to a hospital for a battery of tests and he scheduled an appointment for his patient.

On the appointed day, Willard went with Jeff to St. Vincent's hospital where Jeff submitted to a series of tests. He had everything, a CAT scan, a brain scan, an MRI and an X-ray, blood work and a urine analysis— fortunately the full moon was weeks away so Jeff's urine was still yellow and had not turned purple yet. The test results revealed absolutely nothing. By all accounts there was nothing wrong with Jeff, yet he was still weak and tired, losing energy every day.

Medical science was at a loss to explain Jeff Foxlove's mysterious illness. Everyone who knew Jeff was concerned. Even Damon Cudmore was worried because he knew that Jeff was sinking and feared that his entire werewolf campaign was about to go down the toilet. He knew he had to do something but he didn't know what.

As if all this wasn't tough enough on poor Jeff, he was plagued with incessant calls from his girlfriend, Dixie. Since his return from the Yucatan, Jeff had gradually stopped seeing her. He simply didn't have the energy for romance. In addition, he felt that as long as he was secretly half man, half beast, they could have no future together, and as such, he felt that it wasn't right to continue their relationship.

His deep, dark secret was something no one close to him could ever know. It was a secret that plagued him and he wished that he could open up and somehow tell someone.

But how do you tell a woman whose IQ is measured in negative numbers that you have a vicious monster lying dormant inside of you? Dixie had trouble understanding how Jello hardened, so how could she or anyone else possibly understand how a man could turn into a werewolf in the light of the full moon? He couldn't even understand how his complexity had developed and he knew that there was no way he could explain his bizarre condition. As long as he was cursed with this terrible affliction, he felt it best to avoid any friendships at all.

This sudden cooling of their relationship disturbed Dixie, partly because she now had to spend many weekends at home alone, but mainly because she knew that Jeff was her one and only key to stardom. Without Jeff, her movie career was at a standstill and that distressed her.

It was true that Dixie's career was at a standstill, but far more serious was the fact that Jeff Foxlove was slowly withering and dying. With each passing day, he got weaker and more pallid. Life was ebbing out of his body and it seemed that there was nothing anyone could do to stop the process.

CHAPTER 14

It was Willard who finally found out the cause and eventual solution of Jeff's malady and he found that out quite by chance. One day he was up in Harlem with the film crew and they were shooting a commercial for a hair-straightening product. When it came time to wrap, Willard helped the crew put the gear into their truck. As he was doing that, he glanced over his shoulder and happened to see a sign on the building across the street. It read:

Madam Esmeralda, psychic and clairvoyant, answers all your questions.
She sees all, she tells all.
She advises you on matters of the heart and pocketbook.
She is an expert on matters of the occult.

Readings $10.

Willard looked at that sign for the longest time and he thought to himself that maybe this Madam Esmeralda might be the person to know something about werewolves—after all, werewolves were part of the occult—and if she knew about those things then maybe she could tell what was happening to Jeff and why his condition was slowly deteriorating. Maybe she was just a big phony, but then again maybe not, and Willard figured that a consultation was worth a try.

When the truck was loaded, he told the guys to go back to the agency without him, adding that there was something he wanted to do while he was in the area. As soon as the van left, Willard walked across the street, entered the old building and climbed the rickety, dilapidated stairs to the second floor where Madam Esmeralda's studio was located.

He stood before her door but was hesitant to knock because he was seized with pangs of ambivalence. Deep down, he wanted to talk with her and maybe find out about the strange malady that afflicted Jeff. On the other hand, he was afraid of appearing foolish.

After all, how do you tell a perfect stranger that your friend is a werewolf? And how do you ask a fortune teller for a remedy to make a sick werewolf well?

He stood there in the hall before Esmeralda's door for the longest time, debating with himself whether he should knock and talk to the woman and maybe risk ridicule or if he should play it safe and go home. He was painfully shy about meeting Madam Esmeralda, but on the other hand if he went home, he would never know if this fortune teller could, or would, effect the cure for Jeff's lycanthrope malady.

This psychological wrestling match continued for at least fifteen minutes before Willard finally summoned the courage to knock on Madam Esmeralda's door.

Inside, Madam Esmeralda was lounging in a big overstuffed chair watching *Dr. Phil* on television and she was totally unaware of the little man standing in the hall who finally got up the courage to knock on her door. When she heard the knock, Esmeralda called over her shoulder, "Who is it?"

"Madam Esmeralda," replied the meek Willard, "I've come to consult you about a serious problem."

Immediately Esmeralda knew that she had a paying customer and a mental cash register rang in her head. She shut off the television with her remote and jumped up to get into her working garb. First, she slipped into a large black satin robe that was decorated all over with gold-embroidered signs of the zodiac. She wrapped a black-and-gold silk scarf around her head to create a kind of make-shift turban. To this ceremonial regalia, she added numerous gold chains around her neck and a gold ring on each finger.

Thus, properly attired for her role as seer into the realm of the mysterious and unknown, she walked to the door and threw it open with a flourish. She was surprised to see that standing there before her was the small, slight man with a tiny nose and big ears, and a mop of unruly, sandy brown hair. To Esmeralda he looked like an overgrown mouse.

The two figures who now faced each other presented a study in contrast. On one side of the threshold stood delicate Willard only five-foot two inches tall. Confronting Willard on the other side was the colossal Madam Esmeralda who stood six-foot tall and weighed in at almost four hundred pounds in her stocking feet. Willard's first impression was that she was a human mountain covered in an outlandish costume of black and gold fabric.

For a long moment, neither figure spoke but simply stood there looking back at the other while at the same time trying to decide what it was that they were looking at. The contemplation and silence was mutual. It was Esmeralda who first broke the mood.

"You have come to consult Madam Esmeralda, yes?"

Willard nodded timidly, then said, "Yes, I need to ask you about a problem that—"

"Follow me," said Esmeralda and, in a supremely dictatorial manner, turned to lead the way into her parlor. Willard dutifully followed in the wake of the elephantine figure, noticing that the woman's butt seemed even wider than a Mack truck. They walked into the inner sanctum of the soothsayer's domicile.

Once inside, the two sat on opposite sides of a round table. Madam Esmeralda immediately reached out and grabbed Willard's hand leaning over to scrutinize the road map of lines in his palm.

"Ah," she said knowingly, "I see you have a strong life line. You will live a long and happy life. Now your love line—"

Willard abruptly withdrew his hand.

"Please Madam Esmeralda," he said. "This isn't about me. It's my friend who has the problem. It's him I want to talk to you about."

"Oh! In that case I'll need my crystal."

She opened a drawer to a cabinet that stood beside the reading table and she pulled out a five-inch globe of clear glass. This she placed on a black pedestal in the middle of the table. Now this pedestal had a hollow center positioned directly over a hole in the center of the table top. A small light fixture with a red bulb was mounted directly under the hole in the table.

Madam Esmeralda waved her hands around the crystal, making magical gestures while she muttered an assortment of vague mystical incantations. At the same time, she activated a floor switch with her foot. The switch turned on the small light under the table. The effect was that when she uttered her chant, the crystal suddenly came to life and glowed with a mysterious red luminosity.

Normally this burst of mystical razzle-dazzle would draw exclamations of awe from any one of her usual clients, but Willard just sat there silently without expression.

Undaunted, Madam Esmeralda continued with her act.

"Ah yes," she said. "Now the clouds of mystery are parting. The image of your friend is emerging. I am beginning to see his face. And everything is getting clearer. I can see him—"

"Please Madam Esmeralda," said an exasperated Willard. "I don't think there's any need for the crystal ball. I just want your advice about my friend. I want to know if you know anything at all about...well, I don't think the crystal ball is necessary."

Madam Esmeralda twisted her face into a sour expression because she felt that the little mouse-man across the table was beginning to cramp her style. She was just warming up to a dramatic presentation and he'd put a damper on it. With an expression of undisguised disgust, she put the crystal ball back in the drawer, switched off the table light and leaned back in her chair. Her expression changed from theatrical benevolence to harsh seriousness.

"Okay Mouse, suppose you tell me what this is all about. What is it you want to know?"

"Well, you see it's like this," began Willard. "I have this friend who is a werewolf and he—"

Madam Esmeralda suddenly exploded and jumped up from her seat. It was as if the mountain of a woman had suddenly turned into an active volcano.

"What? Werewolf! What the hell are you trying to pull, Mouse? Is this some sort of a joke? Because if it is, I'll flatten your little mouse face and I'll twist the ears right off your head."

"No, no!" said Willard, trying desperately to calm the agitated mountain of a woman and reassure her that he was serious. "No, this is no joke. I'm serious, and everything I say is true. I really do have a friend who is a werewolf and he needs help. Please listen to me. This is no joke, I swear."

Something in Willard's supplication, his pathetic demeanor, his sad but serious eyes, the earnest plea in his voice, calmed the volatile Esmeralda. She plopped back into her chair with a tremendous thud and looked squarely back at the cowering Willard. There was a full minute of silence while she studied him. After a moment of contemplation, she decided that the little mouse-man might be a crackpot but at least he was a sincere crackpot, so she might as well give him the benefit of the doubt and listen to him.

"All right, Mouse. Go ahead, tell me about your werewolf friend, but this had better be good."

Willard cleared his throat and got ready to speak, but before he could get a word out, Esmeralda held up her hand.

"Wait a minute Mouse. Something tells me that this is going to be a long story. Let me get a brew to wet my whistle before you start."

Esmeralda pushed herself back from the table, rose, and lumbered into the kitchen with the gait of a hippopotamus. She opened the refrigerator and grabbed a can of beer.

"Hey," she called out from the kitchen. "I'm gonna have myself a beer. You want one?"

"No thank you, ma'am," replied Willard.

Madam Esmeralda came back to the table with the can of beer in her hand. She threw off her turban and loosened her robe, exposing a pair of skin-tight jeans and a tee-shirt with a *Grateful Dead* logo emblazoned on it, then she plopped herself back in the chair with a resounding thud and opened the can. A spray of beer shot up from the can and spattered the ceiling, adding speckles to the motley pattern that already covered the area above her chair.

Willard waited patiently while Esmeralda took a deep swig of beer and then put a small, black, twisted cigar between her lips. The big woman lighted the cigar, took a drag and blew a cloud of smoke into the air above her head. Then she took another swig of beer. When she was sufficiently fortified, Esmeralda leaned back in her chair and looked directly at Willard.

"Okay Mouse, I'm all ears. Now tell me about your werewolf friend."

Willard then proceeded to tell Esmeralda all about Jeff: how he came to become a werewolf, how he changed at the full moon, how they kept him caged up so that he wouldn't roam about and kill someone, and how recently he'd become sick with some mysterious illness. He told her how they took him to seek medical help; but the doctors were unable to find anything wrong with him, and in spite of all their efforts, Jeff's condition continued to grow worse.

Willard told Madam Esmeralda everything—well, almost everything; he didn't mention how Cudmore was using Jeff the werewolf to make commercials, but then he didn't think that was pertinent to the problem at hand. When Willard had finished, he looked back at Esmeralda for her reaction.

At first Esmeralda said nothing. She just looked at Willard with her piercing eyes and considered all the things he had just told her. In her mind she was weighing the content of his narrative, the descriptions he gave, the details that he presented, all the while trying to determine if the mouse-man had just told the truth or if he had fabricated it as a figment of his weird little imagination. Finally, she spoke.

"Well, that's the damnest thing I ever heard. You didn't just make that up? You're not shitting me?"

"No ma'am, I assure you that every word of what I just told you is the absolute truth. Honest!"

"Yeah, well, the odd thing is that I believe you. I really think that cockamamie story is true." She paused then looked back at Willard gravely. "The only problem is that I can't help you. I don't know a damn thing about werewolves."

"Oh," said a crestfallen Willard, "I was hoping that you could, that maybe you might know something about werewolves. I'm sorry that I troubled you."

A downcast Willard stood up to leave.

CHAPTER 15

Willard had barely turned and taken a step toward the door when Esmeralda called out to him.

"Now wait a minute, Mouse. I said that I didn't know anything about werewolves, but I might know somebody who does."

"You do?"

Esmeralda nodded. "Yeah, I just might."

"Who?"

"Grandma Poopootang."

"Grandma Poo...poo...tang?" Willard repeated the name slowly, unsure that he heard it correctly. "Who is that?"

"She's my grandmother."

"And you think she can help me? Does she know anything at all about werewolves?"

Esmeralda shrugged. "I can't be sure, but she originally came from the islands, maybe nearby the region that your friend visited. She was born and raised on one of those islands, I don't know which one exactly, but I do know that she lived there a long time."

"How long?"

Esmeralda shook her head doubtfully. "I'm not sure about that either, but I know it was for a very long time. You see, I don't really know how old she is, but judging by the look of her, I'd say she goes way, way back. Yeah, she's old all right. Oh hell! I wouldn't even be surprised if she was standing on the shore when Columbus landed."

"But she knows about werewolves?" asked Willard excitedly.

Esmeralda shrugged again. "I don't really know that either. If she does, she never mentioned it to me. But she told me that she was once a voodoo priestess. She knows all about spells and incantations and magical concoctions. She grew up in the Caribbean and knows all the legends and superstitions and mumbo-jumbo from all over that area. If there is anything to that werewolf legend then she would probably know about it."

"Do you think that I could go and talk to her?"

Esmeralda shook her big head. "Nahh! She doesn't talk to strangers. If you showed up at her door she'd tell you to go away and get lost; and she'd probably put a hex on you as well. Believe me, you wouldn't want that."

Willard was stymied for a minute, then he had an inspiration and his mood brightened.

"Well, maybe you could go and see her for me."

"Ahh Mouse!" cried Esmeralda with an expression of genuine pain. "You don't know what you're asking. I hate going out to her place. First of all, it's way far out in the middle of nowhere, in the most deserted part of the city. Second, she's always got some witches brew cooking on the stove and the stuff stinks up the whole house.

"And as if that's not bad enough, whenever I visit, she insists that I have some of her home-made tea and that stuff is dreadful. I have to hold my nose just to drink it and the stuff tastes like she got it from the toilet. Then on top of that, she insists that I eat some of her disgusting, home-made cookies. I can't refuse. She won't take no for an answer. So, I can never get away without eating at least two of her god-awful cookies.

"The cookies and tea taste like hog shit. And that nauseating taste stays in my mouth for days. Sometimes I think the only way to get rid of it is to gargle with Liquid Plumber. Mouse, I just can't face going out there."

"Couldn't you just call her?"

"She ain't got no phone. The only way to talk to her is in person."

"Please Madam Esmeralda," pleaded Willard, "please go and see Grandma Poopootang for me. I'll give you extra money if you will."

At the sound of the word, *money*, the mental cash register rang in Esmeralda's cranium. She looked hard at Willard.

"You'll pay me extra?"

Willard nodded.

"How much extra? How much are we talking about here?"

"Well, I have fifty dollars; I could give you that."

"In cash?"

Willard nodded again.

"No checks?"

Willard shook his head. "No checks. Fifty dollars in cash."

"Let me see the color of your money."

Willard produced his wallet and pulled out two twenties and a ten. He laid the three bills in a row on the table before Madam Esmeralda. Now Willard knew that he was taking a chance by offering this money to the fat fortune teller because it really didn't belong to him. The money came from the petty cash fund at the Cudmore Agency and it was given to him in case he had to deal with any unforeseen expenses during the day's photo session. Since there were no expenses, he would be expected to return all of the money to the petty cash fund.

If he couldn't account for the money the next day, then he would have to make it up out of his own pay. Willard knew that by giving the money to the hippopotamus woman he was taking a calculated risk because Mr. Cudmore might not allow this as a legitimate expense. At the same time, he felt that it was a risk worth taking because this seemed like the only way to find out how to cure Jeff's inexplicable werewolf-malady.

Madam Esmeralda looked at the two twenties and the one ten laying on the table before her and saw that they were genuine. After a moment of contemplation, she announced, "Okay, Mouse, I'll do it. I'll go out and see Grandma Poopootang tonight. I'll ask her what she knows about werewolves, but remember, I make no promises."

"I understand, Madam Esmeralda. All I ask is that you try."

Esmeralda nodded an acknowledgment and with that she seized the money, folded it, and stuck it down her neck into her bra.

Willard handed Esmeralda a business card. "Here's a card. I've written my home number on the back. If you'll call me after you've seen your grandmother I would appreciate it. Oh, and one more thing."

"Yes?"

"I wonder if you could give me a receipt for the money that I just gave you."

"A receipt?"

"Yes, you see that money came from petty cash and my boss wants me to account for every penny I spend. He's going to wonder what I spent that money for and a receipt would kind of help explain the expense. I hope it's not too much trouble."

For a moment Madam Esmeralda was at a loss. None of her customers had ever asked for a receipt before and she really didn't have any printed forms handy. She looked around wondering what she could come up with.

"Hmm," she said, "I'm not sure what I can give you. Maybe this?"

On a table next to her lay a stack of flyers. These were advertisements of her business that she distributed around the neighborhood. She took one of the flyers off the stack and wrote on the back something to the effect that she had received the amount of fifty dollars in cash for services rendered. She handed this to Willard.

"Here. This is the best I can do."

"Thank you, Madam Esmeralda," replied Willard. "Thank you for everything. I can't wait to get your call this evening."

With that, Willard turned and walked out of Madam Esmeralda's studio. The big, fat woman didn't get up to see him to the door; instead she remained seated at her round table, smoking her small black cigar and drinking her can of beer. As she sat there drinking and smoking, she thought about the deal that she had just made. The fifty dollars that the little mouse-man came up with was a welcome bit of income. It would help pay for some of her monthly bills and that was good, yet at the same time, she knew that she still had to earn that money.

She would have to earn the money by taking the long ride out to see Grandma Poopootang. And Esmeralda shuddered at the thought of seeing her grandmother and entering the gloomy house with the heavy atmosphere and strange odors. But a deal was a deal and Esmeralda was honorable enough to fulfill her end of the bargain, even though she knew that she was going to regret it.

CHAPTER 16

That evening, Madam Esmeralda took the 7th Avenue subway to the end of the line and came up from the subterranean cavern onto the street. From there she walked ten blocks to Grandma Poopootang's house. Esmeralda was not a fast walker because her immense bulk prevented easy, fluid locomotion, so it took her well over thirty minutes to walk those blocks to Grandma Poopootang's house.

The first glimpse of Grandma Poopootang's house was always an unnerving sight because the house was the sole structure on an entire city block that was covered with the rubble from demolished buildings. The demolition was the result of an urban renewal scheme that was designed to rejuvenate an old rundown section of town and replace it with modern buildings. Thus, all the buildings, homes, stores, garages, and even a small neighborhood school were pulverized by the wrecking ball—all except for Grandma Poopootang's house.

When asked why her house was the only one remaining, Grandma Poopootang explained that she put a hex on the demolition crew and rendered them impotent to touch her dwelling. Now of course, skeptics were quick to dismiss the idea of a hex, claiming that it was only superstitious nonsense. Nevertheless, the fact remained that Grandma Poopootang's house was still intact while all the other buildings had been flattened, and no one could come up with a rational explanation as to why that was.

Whenever Esmeralda contemplated that solitary house amidst that vast field of rubble, a veritable no-man's land, she always wondered to herself why her aged grandmother continued to live in virtual seclusion in a desolate area that seemed like it was on the outpost of civilization; but she never voiced that question and the reason remained a mystery.

Esmeralda ambled along that final desolate block moving at her slow, but steady, pace until she finally arrived at the front porch of Grandma Poopootang's dark, old house. With great effort she climbed the twelve steps up to the door.

Now Grandma Poopootang did not have an electric doorbell, so the only way Esmeralda could announce her presence was by manipulating the large iron knocker mounted on the door. As she raised the knocker arm and drove it home against the striker plate, Esmeralda could hear the loud boom reverberate inside the house.

After knocking five times, Esmeralda waited for the old woman to come to the door. Eventually, she heard the sound of shuffling footsteps approaching from within, and then she heard the sounds of chains being undone and locks being thrown back. The concerto of chains and tumblers sounded as if an ancient dungeon door was coming open. The only thing missing was a drawbridge and a portcullis.

Soon the door swung open and Grandma Poopootang's wrinkled face appeared in the opening between the door and the jamb.

"Ah, Esmeralda, my lovely fat one, come to visit your old grandmother, have you? Well, come in, come in."

She pulled the door open wide and Esmeralda stepped inside. Immediately her nostrils were assaulted by the stench from some god-awful brew that Grandma Poopootang had simmering on her stove. Esmeralda had no idea what the concoction was, but it smelled for all the world like fourteen cows had recently died in the kitchen.

Grandma Poopootang ushered Esmeralda into the parlor. The room was dimly lit because Grandma Poopootang used only forty-watt bulbs in each of the two corner floor lamps; but even in the dim light, one could see that the furniture, all worn and antiquated pieces, had several layers of dust, the bottom layer possibly dating back to pre-World War I. Near the ceiling there was a layer of a grayish-brown haze that filtered out from the kitchen where the unholy concoction was brewing on the stove.

Poopootang sat in one chair and she motioned to Esmeralda to sit in an archaic, overstuffed chair directly opposite her. When Esmeralda plopped her gargantuan girth down in the chair, a cloud of dust shot out from the upholstery and billowed up to mingle with the soft layer of haze near the ceiling.

Immediately upon sitting, Esmeralda launched into conversation, hoping that by getting right to point of her visit she could engage the old woman's attention so completely that she would forget about bringing out her cookies and tea. But unfortunately for Esmeralda, it was not to be. Before the fat woman could finish her second sentence, the old lady interrupted.

"Ah, Esmeralda you must have come for some of my herbal tea. I just made a fresh pot. And I also baked some cookies that you must try."

Esmeralda tried to protest, making the excuse that she was on a strict diet, but her words fell on deaf ears. Grandma Poopootang had it firmly entrenched in her mind that Esmeralda would eat and drink her fare and there could be no refusing. The old woman rose from her chair and disappeared into the kitchen. In a few minutes she came back with a tray. On the tray was a large ceramic bowl filled with steaming liquid and next to that was a plate with about a dozen round objects that looked like flattened balls of horse manure.

She put the tray down on the low table and stepped back to watch Esmeralda dig in. Cautiously, Esmeralda reached forward with both hands and grasped the ceramic bowl. Slowly she picked it up and brought it to her mouth. Before she maneuvered it to her lips, she paused and looked into the vessel to see what it was that she was about to drink.

The bowl contained some opaque brown liquid with all sorts of strange flotsam, small leaves, unfamiliar seed pods, bits of bark, and various pieces of debris, floating around the surface. To Esmeralda it looked as if Grandma Poopootang had recently swept the front porch then thrown the sweepings into a pot of boiling water to make this concoction which she called herbal tea.

The brew smelled terrible and Esmeralda hesitated to bring the bowl any closer to her lips, but then she looked over the rim of the vessel to see Grandma Poopootang watching intently for the fat woman to take that first sip and then utter some exclamation of pleasure. Esmeralda wanted desperately to pour the repugnant liquid into a nearby planter; but she knew that she could not because that would greatly displease Grandma Poopootang, and this was an old lady who had the power to put a curse on anyone who incurred her displeasure. There was nothing to do but take a drink of the repugnant liquid.

So, Esmeralda gamely took a sip of the abominable brew and found that it tasted even more disgusting than it looked. Swallowing the stuff was incredibly unpleasant. As she felt the foul liquid course down her esophagus through the lower portals of her body and into her stomach, she truly believed that her innards were being instantly mummified. After that first swallow, Esmeralda looked back at Grandma Poopootang with a weak smile.

Satisfied that her tea was appreciated, Grandma Poopootang pushed the plate of horse-manure style cookies forward. With great reluctance, Esmeralda picked up one of the strange cookies brought it to her mouth and took a bite. She shuddered as her teeth crunched into the morsel. It had the consistency of coarse, compacted sand mixed with straw fibers and it tasted like the ingredients from a compost heap.

Esmeralda chewed and chomped, trying to pulverize all the crystalline particles and break up the straw fibers while at the same time moistening them with saliva so that it would all soften into some sort of a digestible paste. The result was that she made a mass of mush in her mouth that she swallowed only with the greatest difficulty. Unfortunately, after she had masticated and swallowed the unpleasant glob, her mouth was bone-dry, and Esmeralda had to take another sip of Grandma's vile tea just to irrigate her gums and palate. At the same time, she managed to chew with her mouth open so she was able to surreptitiously drop a load of crumbs on the handkerchief that was spread across her lap.

That done, Esmeralda figured that it was now time to broach the subject of werewolves. She looked directly into Poopootang's face and began the tale of the little mouse-man who came to her with a story about his lycanthropic friend.

CHAPTER 17

As Esmeralda was telling her story, she looked carefully and intently at Grandma Poopootang for any signs of reaction or feedback. She watched the old woman's withered face for some indication that her words were penetrating or that the old woman was even listening to her. But there was nothing. No reaction whatsoever.

In fact, there were moments when the old woman was so still and lifeless that Esmeralda suspected that Grandma Poopootang had silently suffered an apoplectic stroke and had lapsed into some sort of weird catatonic state. But then, as Esmeralda continued to look at that old brown face, with wrinkled skin the color and texture of a weathered coconut, she became fixated on Grandma Poopootang's eyes.

Those eyes were so clear and bright that they appeared to be almost incandescent in the dim light of the parlor. And as Esmeralda gazed into those eyes, she recognized that deep within the old woman's shriveled frame there burned a vitality and energy that was as alive and fresh as the day that it first sparked.

Esmeralda talked on about Willard and his werewolf friend. She repeated everything that Willard had told her and when she finished, she waited for Grandma Poopootang to say something. She was curious as to what the old lady would say. There was an extended silence and the old woman's response was a long time in coming. For a very lengthy moment, a moment that seemed like an eternity, the old woman continued to sit motionless, like a statue, totally devoid of any discernible movement save for the occasionally blinking of her eyelids. Finally, she spoke.

"Well, Esmeralda, my lovely fat one, so you want to know about werewolves, do you? I will tell you what you want to know; and while I talk, you sit and listen and you eat and drink."

Those last words filled Esmeralda with dread. The very last thing that she wanted to do was drink any more of Grandma Poopootang's vile tea or eat any more of those dreadful cookies, but she knew that the old woman would not continue unless she did so. So, with an internal shudder, Esmeralda reached for another cookie and gamely bit into it. It turned out that this cookie tasted even more foul than the previous one if that was possible, and Esmeralda gagged but tried gamely to continue eating and drinking. At the same time, she managed to drop more morsels of crumbs on the handkerchief across her lap.

Grandma Poopootang seemed oblivious to Esmeralda's shudders or looks of distaste for the food. Instead, the old woman started to talk about the legends of werewolves in the Caribbean. Her speech was slow and deliberate and Esmeralda listened, at the same time becoming aware to her chagrin that she would have to drink more tea and eat at least two more cookies before the old woman finished her discourse.

That very evening Willard was sitting alone in his apartment. After he'd made supper for himself and washed the dishes, he settled down before the television to watch a ballgame. In the middle of the seventh inning his phone rang.

He picked up the receiver and said, "Hello."

"Is this Wilbert?"

"Willard," he corrected, "Madam Esmeralda, is that you?"

"Yeah, Mouse, it's me. Well, I did what you wanted. I went out to see Grandma Poopootang. You have no idea what I went through just to talk with her. My god! My stomach feels awful–like I just swallowed a brick."

"But did Grandma Poopootang know anything about werewolves? Did you find out anything that could help me?"

"Yeah, she knew a lot of stuff about werewolves, and I think I found out what you want to know. I'll tell you, but believe me, I don't think you're gonna like it."

The next morning when Willard got to the agency, he went right to Mr. Cudmore's office and knocked on the door. The Boss was already in his office. He'd arrived only about fifteen minutes before Willard knocked and was still having his morning coffee snack.

Now, Damon Cudmore was a man who liked to start his mornings slowly by easing into them with coffee and a buttered bagel and quiet time in order to get his thoughts in order and establish his mood. This was his usual morning ritual and he didn't like it when anyone interrupted him before he finished. He assumed that everyone in the office knew this; that it was an unwritten rule, carved in an imaginary stone and binding and inviolate on anyone who worked in the Cudmore Agency.

Thus, when Willard knocked on his door, it was as if the little man was ignoring this ironclad dictum and Cudmore immediately became irritable and cranky at Willard's impertinence. He shot Willard a menacing look hoping to wither him into oblivion, but Willard continued to stand there.

"Yes, Willard, what is it? This had better be important."

"Yes sir. I think it is. Well, at least I hope so. I mean it has to do with something that you're concerned about. That's why I thought that I should tell you first thing."

"Get to the point, Willard!" snapped Cudmore with increasing irritation.

"Yes sir. I believe that I've found out what's troubling Jeff. I mean that I believe I know why he's getting sick."

Suddenly Cudmore's entire mood and expression changed. The irritable, cranky demeanor was instantly replaced by an attitude of curiosity and interest. He pushed his coffee and bagel aside.

"Come in, m'boy and sit down."

Willard walked into Cudmore's office and sat down in a chair that Cudmore had pulled up for him beside his desk. Willard was a little nervous because the big man looked at him with an unblinking intensity.

"You say that you know what is happening to Jeff."

"Yes sir."

"Okay, out with it."

"Well sir, I'm pretty sure—well, somewhat sure—that I know what's happening to him. You see, I talked to someone who knows about werewolves. Well, I didn't actually talk to her, but I did talk to someone who talked to her for me. You see, she doesn't talk to strangers and—"

"Damn it! Willard, get to the point!" thundered an impatient Cudmore. "What the hell is the matter with Foxlove?"

"Well sir, the woman who is the expert said that werewolves have to kill. It's in their nature. It's what they live for. When the full moon comes out, the werewolf must go out and find a victim. He must kill that person because werewolves survive on fresh-killed meat and warm blood.

"By keeping Jeff...I mean our werewolf...caged up, and keeping him from making a kill, we are preventing him from following his natural instincts—in essence, starving him. And we're breaking his spirit and that is causing him to die a slow death."

"Well, I'll be damned," said Cudmore absently.

"I know it sounds strange sir, but..."

"No, it doesn't sound strange at all. In fact, it makes perfect sense."

"It does?" asked Willard incredulously.

"Yes, it does," said Cudmore, then he lapsed into dead silence. Willard looked at his boss to see that the big man was totally lost in thought, so he didn't say anything to break the man's concentration. Willard just continued to sit there and wait. Finally, Cudmore spoke.

"How did you say you found all this out, Willard?"

"Well, I was way uptown with the gang doing a photo shoot, when I saw an advertisement for Madam Esmeralda and—"

"Madam Esmeralda! Who the hell is that? Sounds like some woman who runs a brothel in New Orleans."

"Please Mr. Cudmore," said Willard shrinking from him. "I would never associate with anyone like that. Madam Esmeralda's a fortune teller."

"Okay Willard, don't cringe and wilt away on me. It was just a thought. Go on, tell me more."

"Well, I went to her place and asked her about werewolves. She told me that maybe her grandmother from the islands might be able to. Anyway, Madam Esmeralda went to see her grandmother for me, and got this information."

Cudmore nodded and said, "Yeah, well maybe this is the answer that we're looking for. It's certainly better than anything else we've tried."

While Cudmore was mulling over, Willard gingerly reached into his pocket and pulled out the receipt that Madam Esmeralda had written. Willard unfolded it and laid it on the desk.

"Here sir, I have to give you this."

Cudmore picked it up and looked at it.

"Eh? What the hell is this?"

"That's the receipt that Madam Esmeralda gave me for her consultation fee. I had to use the expense money from the photo shoot to pay her because I didn't have any money of my own. She doesn't use receipts so she signed a flyer. I know it was a lot of money, but it was the only way I could get Madam Esmeralda to travel to her grandmother's."

Cudmore read the advertisement, turned it over to see Madam Esmeralda's scrawl. Willard half expected his boss to reject the crude document as too expensive or maybe as some kind of joke, but Cudmore surprised him by signing it without a word. He handed it back to Willard.

"Here, give this to Madge in accounting and say I approved it."

As Willard rose, Cudmore stopped him. "Willard, you did good."

Willard was elated by this sudden accolade. He rarely ever received praise from his boss and whenever he did, it put him on cloud nine; it made him feel as if he had just become an important person in the Cudmore ranks. He started to leave the office, but then a thought struck him and he turned back.

"Mr. Cudmore sir?"

"Hmm, yes Willard, what is it?"

"What are you going to do, sir? I mean, after what you just heard if you keep Jeff caged up, he'll die. And you can't let him loose on the night of the full moon or he'll kill someone. Either way it looks like someone has to die, and you can't allow that."

"Suppose you let me worry about that, Willard. After all, that's what I'm here for, to run things and solve problems. Believe me, I'll find a solution to this. In the meantime, you just go back to your cubby hole and tend to business as usual. Rest assured, I will think of something. That's what I do best, think!"

"Yes sir. Whatever you say."

Willard turned and went back to his cubbyhole, but doubts still plagued him. They were between a rock and a hard place and even though Cudmore seemed confident that he would find a way out of the dilemma, Willard wasn't so sure that anyone could do anything to help Jeff. They faced a serious unsolvable quandary.

CHAPTER 18

After Willard left him alone in his office, Cudmore leaned back in his chair and stared up at the ceiling. Willard was right: they certainly had a problem on their hands, one that seemed impossible. Nevertheless, he was certain that if he put his mind to it, he could find the perfect solution. After about twenty minutes of concentration, Cudmore came up with what he thought was the way out of their dilemma. It was, if he said so himself, a stroke of genius.

He smiled in self-satisfaction, then reached for the phone, placing a call to the Brooklyn Iron and Steel Works.

Two weeks went by, and to Willard it seemed as if nothing had changed. Cudmore hadn't said anything about what he was going to do regarding their big werewolf problem. Each day Willard intentionally and conspicuously walked past Cudmore's office as many times as possible, hoping the big boss would divulge his grand solution, but there was nothing. Either Cudmore didn't see Willard or he chose to ignore the diminutive man.

Willard also walked past Jeff's cubicle and he glanced in to see how Jeff was doing. Willard didn't like what he saw. He noticed that with each passing day, Jeff was getting noticeably weaker and more emaciated. Willard was sure that if Jeff spent another night caged up during the full moon, it would be his last. Yet the full moon was only three nights away and nothing had changed. It seemed to Willard that Cudmore wasn't going to do anything to help poor Jeff, and Jeff was going to expire, a victim of his curse.

Another day passed, then another, but still there was no change in the status quo. By the third day Willard assumed that Damon Cudmore failed to come up with a workable solution to the vexing werewolf problem. The full moon was to come out that very night, and Willard feared that it was going to be Jeff's last night on earth. It seemed that everyone was powerless to change his fate.

Sometime in the late afternoon, Willard was working in the mailroom, preparing some packages to be sent out, when he heard Cudmore's voice boom out across the office.

"Willard, get your ass in here!"

Willard immediately put down his scissors and tape and ran to answer his master's summons.

"You called me, Mr. Cudmore?"

"Damn right I did. Come on, Willard, I want to show you something."

"Now sir?"

"Yes, Willard, of course now. Do you think I'd call you now if I wanted to show you something a week from now?"

Willard felt a little foolish for having asked the question.

"No sir, I guess not."

"All right then, follow me."

Cudmore led the way to the freight elevator with Willard dutifully following in his wake. Cudmore punched the button to the sub-basement level. Neither spoke as the elevator made its descent to the subterranean cavern below.

Curiosity was getting the better of Willard and he wanted desperately to ask his boss why they were going to the sub-basement and what it was that they were going to see; but when he looked up at Cudmore, Willard saw a look of determination on the big man's face and he knew that any questions on his part would be met with stony silence. Whenever Damon Cudmore had a brainstorm he liked to hold it back, then spring it on his audience with a sudden flourish, and Willard knew that this was just such an occasion. So, he continued to maintain his silence as they rode down in the slow-moving elevator, knowing that sooner or later, Damon Cudmore would reveal everything.

Eventually, the elevator hit the sub-basement level, the doors opened and both men emerged. When both emerged, they walked forward, with Cudmore leading the way to that remote corner where the cage was situated. When they arrived, Cudmore stopped and waved his arm before him.

"Well?" he asked.

Willard looked on in bewilderment.

"It's the werewolf cage, sir."

"You're damn right, it is."

Willard still didn't understand what he was supposed to be seeing.

"But sir, I've seen that cage many times. It's the same as always."

"No, it's not m'boy. There's one important difference. Look carefully and see what's different."

Willard scanned the cage from top to bottom, then he tilted his head to scrutinize the sides of the iron pen, but try as he might, he couldn't see anything different about it.

"No sir, I'm sorry but I don't see anything different."

"Then I'll show you," said Cudmore with a smile. "Watch!"

Cudmore walked forward and extended his arm. He hooked his index finger around one of the bars and gave it a gentle tug. The cage moved forward.

"Sir," said Willard, "the cage is moving!"

"That's right," replied Cudmore with a broad grin of self-satisfaction.

"But how is that possible?"

"Take a look for yourself, m'boy. You just get down there on the floor and look under this damn thing."

Willard did that. He got down on his hands and knees and put his head to the floor to look under the cage and that's when he saw what Cudmore was talking about.

"Sir," he exclaimed, "the cage is on wheels."

"That's right! I had the Brooklyn Iron and Steel Works come over and mount wheels under this damn thing."

"But I don't understand. Why?"

"Ahh m'boy, that is but another example of my genius at work. You see, Willard, I have solved our werewolf problem and I have figured out how we're going to satiate his predatory urges and thirst for human blood."

"How are these wheels going to help Jeff?"

"Well, that is what I am about to tell you, Willard. Now you just sit down on one of those boxes there and I'll reveal to you the wizardry of my brilliant plan."

Willard sat down. Surely what he was about to hear would be mind-boggling in the extreme.

CHAPTER 19

Willard sat on the box, Cudmore bent forward and put his face close to Willard. Then with fiendish delight he started to disclose his master plan.

Cudmore moved closer to Willard. "Tonight, after Jeff gets into the cage, just before the full moon is up and before he has turned into his wolf form, we're going to roll that cage into a waiting van. Then we'll drive it downtown to my brother's agency. We'll take the cage up in the freight elevator to the fourteenth floor where the Triumph Agency is.

"Now once we get the cage up there, we'll open the door and when Jeff turns into a complete wolfman we'll let him run into the office and find a victim to satiate his animal lust. Brilliant, is it not?"

Willard sat there totally shocked at the audacity of the scheme. He wasn't sure how, but he knew that he had to talk his boss out of attempting to launch this wild venture.

"But Mr. Cudmore, sir, it will be late at night and the offices will be vacant. Everyone will have gone home."

If Willard had hoped to deflate his boss's fiendish plan, he was mistaken. Cudmore remained undeterred.

"Not at all, Willard m'boy; I happen to know that my brother Pythias has a presentation scheduled tomorrow for an important client. There'll be someone in the office burning the midnight oil getting the presentation ready. Rest assured there will be fresh meat ready for the taking tonight."

Willard was aghast. He could not believe all that he'd just heard and for a minute he was speechless. Finally, he found his voice.

"But…but…Mr. Cudmore, you can't do this."

"Why not?"

"Well…it's not right," stammered Willard. "The werewolf will kill someone."

"Of course," replied Cudmore, totally unperturbed. "That's the whole idea behind the plan."

"But sir, that would be murder."

"No, it wouldn't. It would be part of nature. It's like animals in the jungle. When a tiger kills a wild pig, it's not murder; it's part of the natural order of life. It's the same here, there's no difference."

"But sir, there is a difference; it's not the same thing. This isn't the jungle."

"Course it is. It's the advertising jungle and it's just as savage and hostile as anything you'd find in Africa or Asia. So, what we're dealing with here is the law of the jungle and anything we do here is fair play."

"But, we're talking about people at the Triumph Agency. Those are real, live human beings that we are dealing with and killing one of them would be murder. With all due respect, sir, your example isn't valid because we're not talking about pigs being killed!"

"The hell we're not, Willard!" thundered Cudmore. "Have you seen the creatures that work for my brother? They're inhuman, they're sub-creatures, cretins, the scum of the earth. Most of them are no better than pigs. If our wolfy-boy kills one of them, it wouldn't be murder; it would be more of a service to humanity."

Willard listened to every word. He saw the intensity in the big man's face, yet he still couldn't bring himself to believe what he was hearing. Could Damon Cudmore actually condone the slaughter of an innocent human being or was he joking?

"But sir," Willard said. "If someone asked your brother about the people who work for you, he would say the same thing about us."

"Course he would," snapped Cudmore. "That's because the man is an unscrupulous son of a bitch. He doesn't know the meaning of the word *integrity*."

Willard was incredulous If Pythias Cudmore was a son of a bitch, and since the two men were brothers with the same mother, then it stood to reason that Damon was also a son of a bitch. Had either of these brothers ever heard the word: *integrity*?

Willard, however, decided not to press the issue because his boss pursued a convoluted track of twisted logic that was uniquely his own. So, he let the big man drone on.

"Okay Willard, you know my plan. Tonight, before the full moon rises we'll come down here and put it into action."

The audacity of Cudmore's plan left Willard in a paralyzed daze. Cudmore, however, paid no notice to Willard's befuddled condition; instead he grabbed the little man by the arm and led him to the elevator. As the elevator slowly rose to the upper levels, Cudmore chuckled to himself with a kind of depraved satisfaction, obviously overjoyed with his diabolical cleverness. Willard, however, did not know what he should do about what was unfolding.

Around 7:00 that evening, Willard was still sitting in his cubbyhole. Earlier in the day, he'd hoped that maybe he could sneak out of the office and go home unnoticed so as to escape involvement with Damon Cudmore's wretched scheme, but he wasn't able to do that. It seemed that whenever little Willard approached the front door, Damon Cudmore was always standing nearby shooting a menacing glance that withered the little mouse-man and made him retreat meekly back to his cubbyhole.

Willard wasn't sure how that happened: was the big boss positioning himself as a blockade just to thwart his escape, or did he just happen by chance to be in the vicinity whenever Willard tried to make his getaway? Well, whatever the reason, Willard knew that his attempts to slither out had been foiled and, like it or not, he was going to be an accomplice, in Cudmore's upcoming werewolf raid.

So, around 8:00 p.m., the offices of the Cudmore Advertising Agency were deserted except for three men: Damon Cudmore, Jefferson Foxlove, and Willard Plotkin. Willard sat nervously in his tiny cubbyhole anxiously awaiting and dreading the summons that he knew was only minutes away. Sure enough, at half-past the hour, the silence of the deserted office was suddenly shattered by the bellowing of Damon Cudmore.

"Willard, get your ass in here!"

Willard swallowed hard. This was the one call that he dreaded most, but Willard had become conditioned over the years—sort of like a Pavlovian dog—to answer the call whenever it came; so, with great reluctance he rose from his chair and obeyed his master's call. He walked down the corridor and dutifully appeared before the big boss who was waiting for him in the doorway of his office.

"You called me, Mr. Cudmore?"

"Damn right, I did. Come on m'boy it's time we got started. Everything's in readiness."

Willard looked around him.

"Where's Jeff?"

"He's downstairs in his cage. I sent him down a few minutes ago so that he would be sound asleep before we started."

"Does he know what we're going to do tonight? I mean does he know that we're taking him downtown to your brother's agency and that we're going to let him loose there?"

"No, of course not. Jeff's got enough problems on his mind. Why burden him with extraneous details?"

"But sir, with all due respect, this expedition is hardly an extraneous detail. I'm still not sure that we're doing the right thing and maybe Jeff should know how we're using him."

"Willard m'boy we're not *using* Jeff. We're only helping nature take its natural course, so don't think of this as right or wrong. Think of this as part of the intricate web of life running its natural course."

Willard, however, was not so easily reassured.

"Yes sir, but if I may be so bold as to point out, it seems to me that there is a moral question here. I mean, is this an ethical thing to do?"

"Ethics, morality! This is the world of advertising; those words have no meaning here. Look Willard, m'boy, let me explain the facts of life to you. Ethics and morality are purely relative terms. They only have meaning within the larger context of events. And tonight, events are rendering them meaningless.

"Nothing is really certain but the laws of nature. Those are the laws that we're working by tonight. It is the law of competition and commercialism that is motivating us and that law is as strong as that of gravitation. This is an organic system we are dealing with, one that has inexorable laws, laws that we must submit to. Now do you understand?"

Willard was totally confused. To him this certainly seemed like convoluted reasoning, and he didn't understand where the organic system came in or why they were faced with inexorable laws. Unfortunately, he didn't have the power or courage to argue with the forceful, man standing before him.

"Well maybe sir, but I still think that—"

"Willard! Don't think. You're not getting paid to think. Let me do the thinking; that's what I'm good at."

Willard wanted to say that if this plan was an example of Damon Cudmore's style of thinking, then it left a lot to be desired. Unfortunately for him it was not in his nature to voice an objection. He just stood there trying to think up some sort of excuse to extricate himself from this diabolical scheme, but somehow his timid little mind seemed unequal to the task.

Cudmore looked down and saw the sullen, uncertain look on the little man's face.

"Hey, cheer up, Willard! Don't be so gloomy and doomy. Remember, you're in the advertising game and this is what advertising is all about: creativity, ingenuity, and competition. Rising to whatever challenges pop up; that's the spirit! So, come on, let's get started, time's a-wasting. We can't afford to dawdle."

With that, Cudmore grabbed Willard by the arm and led him to the freight elevator. At that point, Willard knew he was an unwilling accomplice in a wicked stratagem concocted by the Machiavellian mind of Damon Cudmore. Cudmore was the picture of supreme confidence, but little Willard had serious qualms about this dubious scheme and how it would turn out. Nevertheless, he allowed himself to be dragged alone, while all the time, wondering what he was about to get into.

CHAPTER 20

Cudmore took long strides to the freight elevator and Willard had to double step just to keep up with him. The two got into the steel compartment, the doors closed behind them, and together they descended to the hidden depths of the building. When they reached the sub-basement level, the doors to the elevator opened, and they walked to the remote corner where the cage stood. Willard immediately saw two brutish-looking characters taping large panels of brown cardboard to the sides of the cage. The front was still exposed and Willard could see the sleeping figure of Jeff Foxlove lying on the floor of the cage.

"Sir, why are those men putting cardboard on the cage?"

"Come on Willard, m'boy; use your imagination! We can't very well move a cage with a werewolf in it about the streets of Manhattan without attracting notice, not even at this late hour. That would arouse suspicion. The cardboard panels will disguise the cage and make it look a big appliance box. If anyone sees us, it will look like we're making a delivery. Clever huh? Do I think of everything or what?"

"Yes sir, you do think of everything…except maybe…"

"Except what?"

"Well, who delivers large appliances at this time of night?"

"Now Willard, let's not get mired in technicalities. This is my plan. I've thought out the whole thing carefully and worked out all of the details. I tell you it's going to work; after all, when has one of my plans ever failed?"

This was a rhetorical question to be sure, but it occurred to Willard that this entire operation was more like a hare-brained scheme than a well-thought-out plan and furthermore, Willard knew that despite the successes of Damon Cudmore's wild schemes many either backfired or else generated unexpected repercussions that negated their success.

But Willard did not voice any objections because he knew that once Cudmore made up his mind to do something there was no dissuading him, and any protest would be brushed aside and construed as dissension in the ranks. Knowing that the wheels were in motion and there was no stopping the dictatorial Cudmore thinking machine, Willard turned his attention to the two louts who were still taping cardboard panels to the cage.

Willard had never seen either of those two goons before. They both had hulking shapes with broad shoulders and long arms. Their short foreheads and large, protruding brow ridges, made them appear more like two prehistoric sub-humans left over from Paleolithic times, and as such, they looked like maybe they belonged inside the cage with Jeff rather than outside.

When the last panel of cardboard was securely in place the two gorilla-men pushed the cage into the back of the waiting van and slammed the back doors to the vehicle. Cudmore turned.

"Okay, Willard, everything is ready. Now you get into the van with Hack and Lug and drive downtown. Get the cage upstairs to the fourteenth floor and let our werewolf do his thing in the Triumph Agency."

Willard blinked back at the big boss.

"But Mr. Cudmore sir, aren't you coming with us? I mean, after all, this is your plan. I should think that you would want to be there just to direct the whole operation and see it carried out."

"Yes, Willard, ordinarily I would go along, but tonight it just so happens that I have some pressing matters upstairs that require my immediate attention. After all, the Cudmore Agency doesn't run by itself; it requires a firm and constant hand at the helm. That's why I'm going to leave you in charge of this expedition. I know that it's a big responsibility but I'm confident that you'll be able to handle it."

"But sir, I really don't think that I'm the man to do this. Shouldn't you get someone who is more qualified, someone who—"

"Come, come m'boy! Now is not the time for false modesty. I've had my eye on you for some time now. I been watching you and I know that deep down you have those rare qualities that make for great leaders. The only thing you've needed is the opportunity to show those qualities. With this, I am handing you that very opportunity. It's up to you to make the most of it."

"Mr. Cudmore, I thank you for your confidence in me, but I really don't—"

"Willard, the time is now. You've got to strike while the iron is hot. This is your widest window of opportunity, the chance to demonstrate your potential. I'm putting you in charge, and it's damn the torpedoes, full speed ahead!"

"Yes Mr. Cudmore," protested the hapless Willard, "but if it's all the same to you, I'd rather not do this."

"Now Willard, let's have no more of this negativity. The full moon is rising and we can't wait any longer."

Once again, Willard found that argument was futile, so he dutifully climbed in the front seat beside Hack who was sitting behind the wheel. Lug then climbed in and pulled the door shut. Willard found himself squeezed between the two brutish men and he knew that like it or not, he was enmeshed in a terrifying scheme and there was no way out.

Cudmore pushed the button that raised the steel door to the service ramp and signaled Hack to get moving. Hack nodded, started the motor and drove the van up the ramp onto the street, where they made a turn toward Lexington Avenue.

As soon as Cudmore saw the van go around the corner from the street and disappear onto Lexington Avenue, he smiled in self-satisfaction, knowing his brilliant plan would soon come to reality. Back in his office he stretched his long frame out on his couch, folded his arms behind his head and promptly fell asleep.

CHAPTER 21

The three men in the front seat of the van drove downtown in glum silence. Willard wanted to say something but he couldn't think of anything and besides, judging by their Neanderthal appearance, he wasn't sure if either of his two companions had ever learned the art of verbal communication. So, Willard continued to sit there mute, squeezed between the two ape-men, all the while hoping that something would happen, that some stroke of divine providence would occur to thwart them from their dangerous and foolhardy mission, but alas for poor Willard, divine providence was asleep and nothing happened.

They arrived at their destination, which was the freight entrance of the building where the Triumph Agency was located. It would seem that Cudmore's nefarious scheme was unfolding just as he had envisioned it. But then again, maybe not. Willard had a brief moment of silent elation when the van pulled up to the freight entrance. He saw that the steel gate was down. They couldn't get into the building and would have to turn around and go back. A very slight smile of satisfaction formed across Willard's lips as he realized that the team must abort their mission.

Willard's euphoria was short-lived, however, because Hack gave a short tap of the horn and a minute later the steel gate cranked up, opening the entranceway. As he drove the van to the loading dock, Hack exchanged silent nods with a man who stood by the control buttons that operated the overhead gate, and Willard understood that Damon Cudmore had had the foresight to grease a few palms to make his plan work.

The loading area was big enough to allow Hack to turn the van and back it against the dock. He shut off the motor and the three men got out of the van. Hack and Lug opened the doors to the van.

The cage was still concealed by the cardboard panels, so Willard was not able to peek in at Jeff. He assumed that Jeff was still asleep in his human form because the full moon had not yet risen in the sky. Soon, however, that would change; the moon would rise and Jeff would awaken and change into his animal being. Willard hoped that they would be in a safe secure place before that happened, lest they become the wolfman's next victims.

Willard stood by and watched as Hack and Lug maneuvered the cardboard-covered cage to the freight elevator, and when the doors opened they pushed it in. Then they rode up to the fourteenth floor. So far, it seemed like everything was going according to Damon Cudmore's diabolical plan. Willard glanced from Hack to Lug and back again. Both men seemed calm and passive as if delivering a werewolf to the scene of a massacre were the most natural thing in the world. Willard, however, felt an uneasy churning inside of his stomach. He wished that he had never gotten involved in this crazy venture. Maybe it would end in disaster for them instead of a Triumph employee.

The elevator arrived at the fourteenth floor. Willard got out and looked around. They were at one end of a short hallway. He could see the glass doors to the Triumph Agency at the other end of the hallway.

By now, Hack and Lug had removed the front cardboard panel and had opened the cage door. Willard looked into the cage and saw that Jeff was still asleep but he was beginning to thrash about. The man-to-werewolf transformation was beginning. In a few minutes there would be no more Jeff Foxlove; in his place would be a ferocious, voracious werewolf, a beast that would be hungry for fresh victims. Willard knew that if he and his two brutish companions did not find a safe hiding place very soon, they would become those victims.

Hack led the way to a nearby stairwell, Lug was close behind and Willard followed in their wake. Inside the stairwell, Lug picked the lock to the stairwell door and opened it. Willard wondered where Lug acquired the knowledge to pick locks. With the door open Hack pulled a massive chain from his backpack. Willard stood by and watched as Hack and Lug fastened the heavy chain around the knob and a nearby pipe. This would presumably secure the door so the wolfman could enter the office but couldn't get back at them.

Hack and Lug worked together in total silence without conversation or making any verbal exchange. Yet they both seemed to know what the other was thinking. It was as if they had some sort of symbiotic relationship that allowed them to communicate on a subliminal level.

As Willard watched the two go about their task, totally oblivious to his presence, the thought occurred to him that up till now, Hack and Lug had managed every phase of the entire operation without any aid or input from him. He was totally superfluous to this entire operation. Cudmore had told him that he was supposed to be in charge of this mission, but so far, he hadn't done or said anything to assert his role as a leader, much less function as an active participant. As Willard continued to stand by and watch helplessly, he asked himself why he had ever been included in this caper in the first place, and try as he might, he could not come up with an answer.

Then again, he thought, maybe it was better that he just stand to one side. Considering the job they were doing, he could always say that he'd only been an innocent bystander during the entire escapade. Well, not exactly innocent, because all of them, Cudmore including, were participating in a major felony. Willard felt, however, that he was the only one who was aware of that fact. Everyone else seemed to be going along with the plan as if they were setting up a picnic in the park.

Hack and Lug had fastened the chain in place and now all they could do was stand by and wait. They didn't have long for that. Suddenly there was a long howl that sent a chill down Willard's spine. He knew that Jeff's metamorphosis was complete, and that he was now a wolfman. He sprang from the cage and passed through the doorway into the office hallway.

Willard turned to look at Hack and Lug to see their reaction, but they had assumed relaxed positions, one leaning against the wall, the other sitting on the floor, both impassive, apparently unperturbed by the fact that a vicious beast, hungry for fresh human blood, was in the hallway, only a few feet away from them.

Willard stood still and listened, trying to guess what was happening next, but for the next few moments all was silent. Willard was consumed with curiosity wondering what was happening, but there was only that eerie silence. Had the werewolf made his way into the Triumph Agency? Curiosity got the better of Willard and he edged his way to the door to look through the gap and take a peek. This proved to be a mistake because the werewolf had not gone very far. He was standing in the hall only a few feet from the cage, sniffing the air and looking around for prey.

That's when he saw Willard's little face looking through the gap in the stairwell door. The beastman let out a low, menacing growl and leapt for the door. Willard backed away just as the creature hit the door with a crashing thud. The wolfman put all his immense strength against the door trying to force it open and get at the potential victims on the other side. In spite of all the beast's efforts and immense strength, the door and the chain held. Willard let out a breath of relief.

The wolfman continued pounding at the door. The robust chain showed no signs of giving way. The doorknob, however, was another matter. Willard looked with increasing apprehension as he saw that the shaft was starting to bend from the enormous pressure and battering exerted by the powerful creature on the other side.

If the barrage continued, the doorknob would break away and the door would fly open. Then they would be in the clutches of the werewolf. He watched with increasing apprehension as the relentless battering continued. The doorknob continued to hold, but it was obvious that it was weakening and wouldn't last much longer. Suddenly, it seemed as if Cudmore's calculated game plan had hit a snag and the perpetrators were about to become the victims.

WEREWOLF ON MADISON AVENUE

Willard edged closer to the stairs, positioning himself for a fast getaway should the wolfman break through the door. Now Willard was fully aware that he could not ever hope to outrun a powerful werewolf, but then he reasoned that he wouldn't have to run that fast. All he would have to do was run faster than either Hack or Lug.

Just when it seemed that the worst was about to happen, and the door was about to yield, there was a sudden and unexpected pause. The pounding, the battering, the growls and howls ceased, and all was quiet. What was happening now? Was this some sort of trick or was the werewolf pausing to regroup before beginning a fresh assault? Willard waited but still there was nothing, no sound, no movement. All remained quiet for what seemed liked the longest time.

Finally, Willard got up the courage to move closer to the door and sneak a peek through the crack at the jamb. When he looked, he saw… nothing! He maneuvered around trying to get another angle so he could see farther into the hall; but try as he might, he didn't see any signs of the wolfman. It was as if the wolfman was gone, as if he had suddenly disappeared!

Then Willard heard a loud crunch and a snap. He couldn't see, but he guessed what had happened. Something, or someone, inside the Triumph Agency had caught the attention of the werewolf, and the creature had changed his tactics to go after other, more accessible prey. The snap and crunch were the sounds of the beast forcing open the locks on the glass doors to the office.

Willard craned his neck and angled his face against the stairwell door to get a better look through the crack. With this new posture, he managed to get a glimpse of something more. Willard could see that the glass doors were open and now the beast was presumably inside and on the prowl for a victim. Damon Cudmore's diabolical plan was back on track.

CHAPTER 22

It was late at night at the Triumph agency, and almost everyone had gone home for the evening. Three people were still around burning the midnight oil. Two of them were in the accounting department going over the books. Another fellow was working alone in his cubicle in the art department on the other side of the floor.

The solitary figure in the art department was an art director by the name of Adrian Lander. It had fallen to him to prepare the mock ups, aka the comprehensives, of the ads that the agency was going to exhibit in the big presentation the following morning. Earlier in the day, when he started assembling the pieces for the presentation, Lander had assumed that he would be finished by five. As he started putting everything together, however, he began to realize that the job would take him into overtime. Even so, he assumed that he would be able to finish his task in the early evening and still be home by 8:00 p.m.

Unfortunately, the job proved to be more complicated than he'd first imagined, and by 8:00, he found that he still had a long way to go. It wasn't until 11:00 p.m. that he began to see a dim light at the end of the tunnel. By then, he was finally finishing up the last piece. He printed the final ad and all that remained was for him to mount it on illustration board, cover it with a sheet of acetate, then matte it. After that, the entire job would be finished and he could go home and hit the sack.

Lander's cubicle was far from the entrance doors and he was running the printer when the werewolf forced his way through the outer glass doors. The hum of the machine drowned out the crunch and snap of the office doors being forced open. Adrian Lander didn't know it, but at that moment a hungry werewolf, was on the premises and prowling for prey.

On the other side of the floor, in the accounting department, Otto Pleisner, the chief accountant at Triumph, and his assistant Ambrose Tweak, were also working diligently. Both men were busy analyzing and organizing the company accounts. Pleisner was poring over the books, receipts, and tally sheets, and Tweak was sitting before his computer entering numbers on spread sheets.

Pleisner was the older of the two men. He was a dedicated and fanatical bookkeeper who often became so engrossed in numbers and so consumed in his books and spreadsheets that he lost all track of time—totally oblivious to his surroundings. Such was the case this night.

His assistant, Tweak, was less dedicated and far less enthusiastic. He was restless at his computer and after working all day and into the night, he wanted to call it quits for the day; but he knew that they could not do that until his boss, the obsessive Mr. Pleisner, had added each column of figures and verified every bottom line. Only when the older man was completely satisfied that all the numbers were perfect in every detail could they turn out the lights and go home.

Pleisner's attention was completed focused on his numbers and he didn't hear the sounds when the entrance doors were forced open. Tweak, however, did hear the crunch and snap as the locks were broken. He turned back to his boss.

"Mr. Pleisner, did you hear that?"

Pleisner, his attention still on his books, returned, "What Ambrose? Did I hear what?"

"I heard a cracking and popping noise just now."

"I didn't hear it; but it was probably the sound of the building air conditioners shutting down."

"No, they shut off the air conditioners hours ago."

"Well, I wouldn't worry about it, the pipes and ducts in these big buildings often make sounds at night. Get back to your spreadsheets Ambrose, and let's have no more distractions."

"Yes sir, but first I have to go to the bathroom."

"Well then, go and be quick about it so you can finish."

"Yes sir," Ambrose replied meekly. He got up from his desk and headed for the men's room.

In the men's room, Ambrose Tweak answered the call of nature then washed and dried his hands. As he was leaving the men's room, he was greeted with a sight that completely unnerved him. There at the end of the corridor was a strange, hairy animal-like creature walking upright like a man. Ambrose stood frozen in place as he tried to figure out what kind of beast he was looking at.

Fortunately for Ambrose, the werewolf had already sniffed fresh blood. The scent was coming from a victim in the art department and the beast was so intent on following the trail that he didn't notice the shocked young accountant standing only ten feet away in the dark corridor. The werewolf passed out of sight into an adjacent corridor leading to the art department, leaving Ambrose Tweak to wonder what it was that he had just seen.

Ambrose sprinted back to the accounting office to tell his boss about the strange creature wandering in the halls.

"Mr. Pleisner, I just saw the strangest sight!"

Pleisner regarded Tweak's exuberant manner as a distraction from his work. He hated distractions, and he tried hard to stay glued to his numbers while at the same time giving token response to the young assistant.

"What, Ambrose? What did you see?"

"Well sir, it's kind of hard to describe, but it was a strange sort of man. Well, that is, it looked and walked like a man, but it had large pointy ears and his face was covered with hair. I mean he was really weird looking."

Without looking up from his numbers, Pleisner replied, "It sounds like creative just hired a new writer. Writers are a strange-looking lot. They never shave or get a haircut—or bathe, for that matter. I wouldn't get too concerned about it, Ambrose. Now return to your work."

"Yes sir," said Tweak and he sat down in front of his computer screen.

At that point the werewolf had just entered the art department. The entire section was dark except for one light that glowed from a cubicle in the far corner of the department. The werewolf sniffed the air and he caught the scent of flesh and blood. His sharp ears captured the sounds of activity emanating from that far corner and he knew instinctively that fresh prey was within his grasp.

The beast climbed up onto the narrow partition separating the cubicles. In a low crouch, with sure-footed stealth and animal agility, he navigated along the top edges of the narrow walls to move ever closer to that last cubicle where the unsuspecting art director was hard at work.

In that distant cubicle Adrian Lander was finishing up his last piece. He had the print-out mounted on the illustration board and had covered it with a clear acetate sheet. He cut the matte, sandwiched the whole thing together, ran flat-black tape around the edges. At long last, he looked forward to getting home.

He didn't realize it then, but death in the form of a vicious werewolf was sniffing his blood, creeping closer and closer along the top of the narrow cubicle partitions and was only a few feet away from where he was working.

When Lander finished taping the edges of the comp, he held it up before him and looked with satisfaction upon his work. For him it had been a long, hard night, but now that he was finished, he felt that it had been worth the effort because he knew he had put together a dynamite presentation.

He was looking on that last board when he heard a low growl behind him. Slowly he turned, wondering what that curious sound was. When he turned and looked up, he was horrified to see a hideous figure crouched on the cubicle wall opposite him. The creature was still shrouded in darkness but Lander could see the outline of its hairy animal form, the long fangs projecting from the snout, and two red eyes that burned like hot coals in the darkness.

Lander stood there, petrified, unable to move, unable to utter a sound. For one long moment, both figures looked at each other without movement then, just when it seemed that Adrian Lander had found his voice and was about to scream, the beast leaped from the wall and plunged his claws into Lander's shoulders and his fangs into the man's neck. Lander tried vainly to struggle but he was caught completely off guard and his puny muscles were no match for the greater power of the werewolf.

In a matter of minutes, it was all over. The werewolf had ripped into the victim's flesh, torn out organs, gorged itself on human flesh and drank the victim's blood. Now the beast raised his head and let out a long victory howl.

Back in the accounting department, Ambrose Tweak heard the commotion and the long howl coming from the direction of the art department. He turned to Otto Pleisner who still had his nose in the books.

"Did you hear that, Mr. Pleisner?"

"What Ambrose? What is it this time?"

"Well there was a loud raucous scream, then something that sounded like a howl coming from the art department."

"From the art department you say? It doesn't surprise me. Those guys are a bunch of party animals. They can find any excuse for a celebration, so they're probably whooping it up now for no good reason. Don't pay any mind to their shenanigans. Get back to work and let's have no more distractions; we're almost finished."

"Yes sir."

And Ambrose Tweak returned his attention reluctantly to the computer.

An hour later, the offices of the Triumph Agency were deserted. The werewolf, satisfied from his night of carnage, had returned to his cage and fallen asleep on the floor. Hack and Lug crept out of the stairwell, locked the cage, then replaced the cardboard front panel. They pushed the cage into the freight elevator and, along with Willard, they descended to the ground level where the van was still parked. They loaded the van and went back to the Cudmore agency.

Otto Pleisner and Ambrose Tweak had also finished their work. They packed up their books and left by the back door and never saw the damaged, glass entrance doors. They never saw the dead body in the art department either. They took the elevator and left the building. The only one who didn't leave was the art director, Adrian Lander. His torn, mangled body still lay in a pool of blood in his cubicle in the art department of the Triumph Advertising Agency. He had finished his last presentation and would never go home again.

CHAPTER 23

The next morning, Pythias Cudmore arrived at his agency on the fourteenth floor. The minute he stepped off the elevator and walked into the reception area, his ears were assaulted by a hubbub and commotion coming from the creative department and that annoyed him. Pythias Cudmore did not like hubbubs and commotion in his agency. He liked peace, quiet, and tranquility. Peace, quiet, and tranquility meant that his employees were working diligently at their desks, totally focused on their assigned tasks.

Unrest and confusion on the other hand, meant that his serfs were distracted and occupied with matters other than their assigned tasks. Hubbub and commotion meant that his peons were not slaving peacefully at work. This was something that Pythias Cudmore could not, and would not stand for, because he truly believed that when he hired someone, he was actually buying their body, mind, and soul totally, for the entire workday. He expected complete dedication from all his employees and demanded their undivided attention to the Cudmore mission. He therefore tolerated no commotions and no disturbances.

When he heard the din coming from his creative department, he immediately marched into the area, fully intending to lay down the law and take his employees to task. The minute the big man came around the corner and into the corridor of the creative department, Bernice Zwart, a petite woman who worked in the media scheduling department, rushed up to him.

"Oh, Mr. Cudmore, it's a good thing that you're finally here. Something terrible has happened."

This unexpected outburst caught Cudmore off guard because he assumed that he would have the first word. He looked down at the small woman and glared into her gerbil-like face.

"What do you mean something terrible has happened. What are you talking about?"

"It's Adrian Lander, sir."

"Yes, well what about him? He's supposed to be working on the Sweetpit Deodorant Campaign."

"No sir, not anymore."

"Whaddaya mean, not anymore? He has to be working on that campaign, we have clients coming this morning to view our presentation."

Cudmore had no idea what happened, but he sensed that his precious presentation was in jeopardy and this agitated him no end. Little Bernice could see that Pythias Cudmore's face was turning crimson and she knew his blood was starting to percolate and that he was on the verge of erupting into a tirade. She hated being around him when he became stressed-out, because then he became irrational and vociferous and usually vented his spleen on the nearest target. Unfortunately, everyone else in the agency shared her fears, so the minute the big boss came into the agency they all disappeared, leaving poor, innocent Bernice to face the tyrannical Cudmore.

Standing in the prime, frontal target position she tried to soothe the big man.

"Well, sir," she began in a timid voice, "it's like this; Mr. Lander can't work on the campaign presentation because…how should I put this? He's dead."

"Dead! Whattaya mean dead?" thundered the uncomprehending Cudmore. "When I left last night, he was in his cubicle working on the comps. He was alive then, how could he be dead now? How dare he die on me when I have clients coming in this very morning!"

Little Bernice could see that her boss was turning into a fire-breathing dragon, stoking up his lungs and on the verge of spraying scorching flame in all directions. She tried her best to pacify his savage nature.

"Well sir, I don't think it was intentional on his part. I mean, it doesn't look like it was his fault."

"Intentional or not," snarled Cudmore, "he's got no business dying on my time. Certainly not in the middle of a presentation."

"Yes sir. I mean no sir! Well, what I mean is that I don't think that he died on purpose. He seems to have been the victim of a vicious attack."

"Attack? What the hell are you talking about?"

"Well, it's kind of hard to explain sir, but if you would take a look for yourself, then—"

"That's exactly what I intend to do."

Cudmore brushed the little Bernice aside and marched down the corridor to the last cubicle where the corpse lay. Bernice ran behind him. Cudmore arrived at the last cubicle to find Myron Needlebaum standing in the opening with his back to the victim."

"Needlebaum, what are you doing here?" asked Cudmore.

"Well sir, I took it upon myself to stand guard and make sure no one disturbed the scene of the crime."

"Good idea." Cudmore looked over Needlebaum's shoulder at the corpse. "Are you sure he's dead?"

Needlebaum was a little flustered by this unexpected question.

"Well, no sir...I mean...that is to say...well sir, I didn't go in and feel the pulse or touch the body or anything like that. I just looked in. But judging by that gaping hole in his chest, and with his throat torn out like that, and all that blood...well, I don't see how he could still be alive. Least ways, he hasn't moved or made a sound since I've been here."

"Quite right. Well, do you know if he finished the comps for this morning's presentation?"

This question caught Myron off guard. "To be honest, sir, I don't have any idea. I mean when I first saw that body, and all that blood, well, my first thought was to stand guard until the police came.

"Damn it, man! The police can wait. We have clients coming in at ten o'clock. They're expecting us to be prepared. Look over there, on top of that cabinet. It looks like a stack of boards. Go in and see if those are the mock-ups."

Needlebaum was a little hesitant. Impatiently, Cudmore brushed him aside and went to the cabinet himself, carefully stepping around the corpse and the pool of blood. He looked carefully at the stack of boards resting on top. After methodically examining each one, he announced, "Yes they're all here. Lander did a good job."

"Yes sir," said Needlebaum dryly, "I'm sure he would be glad to know that he served the Triumph Agency right up to his dying moment."

Cudmore ignored the comment and walked out of the cubicle with the stack of boards in his hands. He handed them to Needlebaum.

"Take these to the conference room and arrange them along the presentation rack."

"You mean, sir, that you're still going ahead with this morning's presentation?"

"Of course, we go ahead with the presentation. That's what we're in business for, to sell advertising. We can't let a little thing like a murder stop us."

"Yes sir, I know that, but what I meant was, what are you going to do about Adrian?"

"Do? Whadda you want me to do about him? He's dead, isn't he? What can I do about that? Whadda you think, that I'm some sort of miracle worker that can raise a corpse up from the dead?"

"Well, no sir, I didn't mean that, but…well, I mean…shouldn't we call the police?"

"Yes, of course. That's what we should do, call the police. Yes, we will call them, but not just yet. It wouldn't do to have a lot of policemen running around while our clients are here."

"No sir, we wouldn't want anything to spoil your presentation."

There was a definite edge of sarcasm in Needlebaum's remark but it flew right past Pythias Cudmore.

"I tell you what, Needlebaum, you call the police right after our clients leave."

"Yes, but that will be hours from now. The police will ask why we waited so long to call them."

"Well, tell them that no one discovered the body till late. After all, this cubicle is on the far side of the floor. It's out of the way, off the beaten path. We can say that no one had any reason to come over here."

"But sir, that would be a lie!"

"Nonsense Needlebaum; there's no such thing as a lie in the advertising world. There's only creative embellishment. Now do as I say, and put those boards in the conference room."

Myron Needlebaum nodded and dutifully went off to the conference room carrying the stack of boards. That left Pythias Cudmore and little Bernice still standing outside the bloodied cubicle. Bernice stood to one side so she could avoid looking in at the grisly scene, but Cudmore, apparently unperturbed by the blood and gore, remained standing in the opening looking back at the red-spattered walls and the wretched corpse lying on the floor in the middle of a pool of blood. For a long moment he continued to stand there, lost in a train of thought. Then he mumbled aloud, to no one in particular, "I'll bet my brother had something to do with this."

Bernice was aghast. She looked up at the big man.

"Mr. Cudmore, that is a terrible thing to say about another human being. How could you even think something like that? And your brother no less!"

Cudmore looked down at her gerbil face.

"How? Because I know my lousy, shiftless brother and I know me. I know I'd do the same to him if I thought I could get away with it. And that's just it. That's what bothers me. I can't for the life of me figure out how he pulled this off, but I'd give the skin off my ass to know how he did it."

"Really Mr. Cudmore, I don't think that anyone, not even your brother would—"

"Never mind. Time's a wasting. When our clients come in, show them to the conference room. After the presentation, you can call the police. In the meantime, keep this thing under wraps."

"Yes sir, I'll try." said Bernice Zwart timidly.

Well, Pythias Cudmore did have his presentation, and later the police did come up to investigate. They wandered and nosed around, questioned everyone on the floor. The CSI team came in and took a multitude of samples. They photographed the corpse and the entire area. Detectives spent a lot of time talking to everyone in the agency. At the end of the day they'd gathered all the evidence that they could, but they still weren't sure what to make of the murder.

This murder had the same MO as the murder in the park a few months ago. Back then, the police assumed that a large animal, possibly a savage dog, had mauled and killed the two victims. It was logical to assume that the same animal had committed this murder. But if this was the case, then the police could not figure out how a large, vicious animal could enter an office building, make it to the 14th floor, break open the doors, kill a victim and escape without anyone seeing the beast.

It was a sensational crime to be sure, but while the investigation was on, the police refused to make any comments or issue any press releases, and Pythias Cudmore managed to keep the news media at bay. So, the horrible details were kept under wraps and the public had no idea that there was a savage beast prowling the streets of Manhattan at night.

138

CHAPTER 24

The morning after the big raid, Willard turned on the television to watch the news. He wanted to see what the media had to say about the horrible murder the night before at the Triumph Agency. He tuned into all the local stations, but was disappointed because none of the programs gave much in the way of information. All they said was that apparently a man had been murdered during the night at the Triumph Advertising Agency and that the police were investigating the incident. At the moment, however, there were no witnesses, leads, or suspects.

Now, in the light of morning, Willard woke up with a feeling of deep guilt hanging over his head. He felt guilty for having allowed himself to be an accomplice in a vicious murder. Moreover, he imagined that he was now a wanted criminal and that at any moment the police would uncover what really happened, and then the long arm of the law would reach out and grab him then throw him into the slammer to be incarcerated for the rest of his life. He sat there alone in his tiny apartment wondering how long it would be before he heard the ominous knock on the door followed by the announcement that the police were outside wanting in.

Glumly he showered, got dressed, and made breakfast. Then he left for work. On the way to work he picked up all the morning papers and when he got to the office he read through all of them hoping to find more information on the crime, but there was nothing. Willard was desperate to find out what the police knew and what was going on up at the Triumph Agency.

The news media wasn't much help, but fortunately, there was another way. It so happened that little Willard Plotkin knew someone who worked at the Triumph Agency. He knew Bernice Zwart. In fact, Willard and Bernice were a kind of clandestine item.

About eight months previous, the two had met at a Zasu Pitts film retrospective being screened at an art house down in the village. There weren't many fans of the incomparable Zasu Pitts at the retrospective, in fact, on the evening of the showing, it turned out that Willard and Bernice were the only two in the audience. And so, it happened that the two came together, and after overcoming their mutual shyness, struck up a conversation.

Now Bernice was not particularly pretty and certainly not sexy-looking. The best anyone could say for her was that she was kind of plain in appearance with a non-descript figure and a cute gerbil-like face. She was not the kind of woman who would attract a man's eye. In fact, she was so plain that men would even ignore her at a drunken frat party. Well, if she was unattractive, Willard was not much better.

But somehow there was a spark of male-female interest that attracted one to the other. A friendship developed and they started seeing each other regularly. Willard with his mouse-like appearance, and Bernice with her gerbil face, began a relationship which had the outward appearance of two large rodents in a sort of mating ritual. But theirs was not a relationship of carefree abandon filled with unbridled animal lust. Quite the opposite. They usually ended their evenings with Willard shaking Bernice's hand and saying goodnight. This was hardly the romantic gesture that would make Bernice's nipples turn hard, but she liked Willard and she felt that if they continued seeing each other then maybe his testosterone level would rise and eventually he would go so far as to plant a kiss on her forehead. At least she could hope for such a moment.

Anyway, after that first meeting at the film retrospective, they began an ingenuous platonic relationship. But oddly, it wasn't until their third date that they learned that each worked in advertising for a rival Cudmore brother.

At that point, they realized they had a problem. They recognized that if either Cudmore brother found out he had an employee who knew someone who worked for his despicable rival brother, then he would press the advantage and use his employee to tap into the relationship for possible nefarious purposes. This might mean that Bernice could become a spy and possibly a saboteur for Willard or vice-versa. Neither one wanted to become an espionage pawn for their boss.

But what could they do? By now they had formed a friendship that neither wanted to terminate, and neither wanted to quit their job. So, they decided to continue seeing each other on the sly, that is, and they would keep their association a secret. With that object in mind, they made a pact that they would never talk shop during their dates and never mention their relationship to others at work. In this way, neither could be accused of using the other as a source for gathering intelligence for his or her agency and no one could use them for infiltration into the enemy camp. That agreement worked for the better part of a year.

Now, however, Willard was in a critical situation; he felt he had to know what was going on at the Triumph Agency and what the authorities were doing about the raid the night before. He believed that his very existence was in jeopardy and it seemed to him that the only way of finding out what was happening was to ask Bernice. Yet, at the same time, he realized that in asking her, he would be violating their sanctified agreement. This troubled him, but right now, she seemed to be his only source for information and he was burning with curiosity; so what else could he do? It seemed to him that he had no alternative but to stage a meeting and try to finesse the information out of her.

He called Bernice that morning, and arranged for them to meet after work. He set up the meeting at one of their usual out-of-the-way haunts, the White Horse Tavern in the West Village. Willard got there first and took a seat in a corner booth. He fretted while he waited for Bernice because he knew that he was about to breach their sacred pact and he felt guilty.

Yet at the same time, he was burning to know if anyone had any inkling as to his participation in the crime so recently committed. Maybe there were witnesses, and if so, he wanted to know if any of them had seen him and his accomplices coming into or out of the building. Maybe he would be violating a trust by using Bernice in this way, but perhaps this once, he told himself, the ends justified the means.

While he sat there in the booth waiting for Bernice to arrive, Willard tried to think of some subtle way that he could broach the subject of the attack without coming right out with a direct question. Maybe he could, with apparent innocence, steer a perfectly innocuous conversation toward the subject of recent crimes in the news. Maybe that would be enough to spark Bernice's imagination so she would jump into the topic that he so desperately wanted to know about. His guilt mounted because he knew that he was going to have to employ some sort of devious tactics to find out what he needed to know and up till now he had always been honest and straightforward with Bernice.

Willard was going over all sorts of possible game plans in his mind when Bernice walked in. Willard was glad to see her but at the same time he gulped with apprehension, feeling that their relationship was now hanging on tenterhooks. When she entered the tavern she looked around, hurried to his booth and sat down. They immediately got their preliminary greetings out of the way, then they ordered drinks.

While they were waiting for the drinks, Willard started to say something, but Bernice cut him off.

"Willard," she said anxiously, "I have to talk to you about something very important. Something dreadful has happened. Something that I must talk to someone about and I think that you're the only one I can confide in. I know that we made a solemn vow never to speak about anything that goes on at the office, but something very strange and very tragic has happened; and I really must talk about it. You're the only friend I can turn to. I'm sorry but I have to break our pact, just this once. I hope you'll forgive me."

Willard was suddenly elated. This seemed to be the opportunity that he was hoping for, and now it was about to drop into his lap. He was energized to hear what she had to say, but at the same time he didn't want to show his excitement lest he give himself away. He sat there and tried hard to maintain his composure.

"Sure, Bernice. If you feel this is something that you've got to get off your chest, then I think you should go ahead and do it. I think that we can bend the rules this once. I'm sure we're both strong enough to cope with this one infraction."

"Oh, thank you, Willard! I knew you'd be understanding." She paused for a minute trying to think of how to go about telling Willard of the murder scene in her office. Willard was dying to hear what she had to say, but he did his best to sit impassively. Finally, Bernice went on.

"Did you hear anything about what happened up at our agency?"

"Well, I think I heard a rumor about some sort of accident that happened in your offices. Is that what you're talking about?"

"Yes, but it wasn't an accident. There was a murder at our place."

"No! Really? What happened?"

Bernice then proceeded to tell Willard all the gory details about how the body was discovered in the morning. Then she described the crime scene.

"What do the police make of it?" asked Willard. "Do they have any leads or suspects?"

"That's the odd thing," said Bernice. "They think it was the attack of some vicious animal."

"An animal! How is that possible? I mean, where could it have come from?"

"Well, that's the puzzling aspect. Judging by the wounds and the hair samples, the police believe it was a wolf."

"A wolf!" Willard tried to sound totally surprised, but at the same time, he hoped that he wasn't overdoing his histrionics.

Bernice didn't seem to notice, and she went on. "Yeah, but if it really was a wolf, the police can't figure out is how it got into the building in the middle of the night and how it got up to the fourteenth floor. Also, the police can't figure how an animal could break the door locks like it did."

"Well, I suppose if a beast were strong and heavy enough, then maybe he could push his weight against the door," suggested Willard feigning innocence.

Bernice nodded. "I suppose that is possible, but then how did the animal get away without anyone seeing him? And where did it go afterward?"

There was a pause in the conversation. Willard could see that Bernice was recalling everything that had happened at her office and at the same time, thinking about the implications of all that she had just said. Willard sat there looking at her, while all the time maintaining his silence lest he say something that might reveal that he really wasn't as innocent as he pretended to be. He continued to sit quietly and wait; after a while Bernice spoke again.

"The odd thing is that this isn't the first time that the police had seen a wolf attack like this. They said that a similar incident with the same vicious attack pattern happened in the park about five months ago."

"Is that right?" Now, Willard was genuinely surprised. This was the first time that he 'd heard anything about this particular incident.

"Yes, it seems that a young couple was sitting in the park at night making out when they were attacked by a wolf.

"A wolf in the park! How is that possible?"

"Well, the police admitted that it is totally unusual, but they figured that maybe the animal migrated from the upstate woods. Since no one ever saw the animal, and since there were no more attacks, the police assumed that it left the city and returned to the woods where it came from. Now, with this new attack at our offices, the police believe that the wolf is still in the city, holed up somewhere."

"Do they know where?"

"No, they have no idea where it could be hiding."

"Have they said what they're going to do now?"

Bernice nodded.

"They said that they're going to increase the number of patrols around the city and are going to be on the lookout for any large animal. The policemen are going to be armed with riot guns and will have orders to shoot to kill.

"They also talked with a zoologist at the zoo. He told the police that animals like wolves often return to the scene of a kill, possibly thinking that there may be more prey nearby. The police are going to station a couple of men at the office just in case. Needless to say, none of us are going to work late anymore."

"No, I would guess not," said Willard.

"Oh Willard, I want to thank you for letting me go on about all of this. I know we said no office talk, but I had to tell someone and I thought that you would be the only one who could understand. Thank you."

"No problem, Bernice. That's what friends are for. I'm glad that I could help."

Willard meant that last part, because now he had found out what he wanted to know, and quite frankly, he was nervous about all he had just heard.

CHAPTER 25

Willard immediately went to back to the Cudmore Agency and proceeded to Damon Cudmore's office. Cudmore was still there, seated behind his desk, working late. When Willard appeared and knocked, Cudmore waved him in. Willard sat down and blurted out all that he'd learned about the police investigation and their findings at the Triumph Agency. He was careful, however, not to mention Bernice Zwart. Nevertheless, Cudmore was curious as to Willard's sources.

"How did you find all this out, Willard?"

Willard suddenly had to think fast. "Well sir, I was in this bar when—"

"You were in a bar, Willard!" Cudmore was genuinely surprised that little Willard would enter a barroom.

Willard was a little disconcerted to find that his boss thought of him as possibly a naïve, innocent—after all he was an adult man, albeit a small, mousy one—and was not totally unsophisticated, although not exactly a man-of-the-world either. Still, he decided to play along and not disillusion Mr. Cudmore.

"Yes sir! You see I didn't have my cell phone with me, and I went into this bar to use the pay phone."

Cudmore nodded but said nothing.

"Anyway, that's when I heard these guys talking. I guess they were all from the Triumph Agency. Well, when I heard them talking about a wild murder up at their offices, I edged closer so I could get an earful of their conversation. That's how I learned all about this."

"Good work, Willard! That's the kind of initiative I like to see."

There followed a few moments of silence. Willard could see that his boss was deep in thought. He waited a few more minutes then finally asked, "Gee Mr. Cudmore, what are you going to do now? You can't bring the cage back to the Triumph Agency because the police will be waiting there. It seems like you're not going to be able to let our werewolf loose anymore."

"Not necessarily, Willard; it's true that we can't return to Triumph, but that doesn't mean that we're stymied. After all, Triumph isn't the only advertising agency in town. There are tons of others. Take Young and Rubicam for example. I never liked those bastards up at Y and R. They always seemed a little too high-minded for my tastes. Serve 'em right if we thinned out their ranks a little."

Cudmore leaned back in his chair and smiled with self-satisfaction. "Yeah, maybe Young and Rubicam should be our next target."

Willard recoiled in shock.

"Mr. Cudmore, you don't mean to say that you're going to continue letting our Jeff, kill innocent people. I really think that—"

Cudmore cut him off. "Willard, I told you before not to think. I'll do the thinking around here. It's what I'm good at."

"Yes sir. If you say so," said Willard timidly.

Willard got up and walked out of Cudmore's office shaking his head in disbelief, then he turned and marched down the corridor straight to Jeff Foxlove's office. Jeff was still in his office sitting before his word processor. Willard entered and sat down, then told Jeff all he had learned from Bernice and of his subsequent conversation with Damon Cudmore. When Jeff had heard all Willard had to tell him, he let out a moan of despair.

"Oh, my god! I can't believe that Cudmore is such a lousy, heartless bastard. He told me at the beginning that he would keep me from killing people."

"It seems that Mr. Cudmore doesn't think that people in the advertising business are really people and so this isn't really murder."

"Yeah." Jeff nodded. "That's easy for him to say because he's not the one killing people. I'm the killer."

"Not really, Jeff. I mean, it's not your fault if you turn into a werewolf each month."

Jeff shook his head. "Maybe not, but that doesn't make it any easier on me. The next morning after a night of being a werewolf, I wake up and I know that I've killed someone. It's a horrible feeling, Willard, and I can't go on like this."

"What are you going to do, Jeff? It looks like Mr. Cudmore is going to keep on doing this for as long as he can get away with it. What can you do to stop it?"

Jeff shook his head. "I really don't know. I'm not sure there's much I can do. It looks like this is the end for me. If I stay in the cage during the full moon I'll gradually wither away and die. And if I go through Cudmore's dirty plan, I'll keep on killing innocent people until eventually I'll be shot down like the animal I am. It's like I'm in a blind alley with no way out."

"Well, at least you have one consolation," said Willard.

"What's that?"

"As a werewolf you can't be killed by ordinary bullets. Werewolves can only be killed by silver bullets."

"How do you know that, Willard?"

"Well...I...er...that is to say, I..." stammered Willard. Willard wasn't sure how he knew that, but for some reason he always thought it to be true.

"You learned that from watching reruns of old monster movies on television, didn't you?"

Willard nodded sheepishly.

148

"Yeah, well," said Jeff, "you can't go by any of that because you really don't know if it's true or not. After all, that's just the figment of some Hollywood writer's imagination. Who knows if there's any basis in fact. I'll wager that there isn't, but I certainly don't want to find out."

Willard nodded, and for a minute neither man spoke. They sat there in a cloud of gloom, not knowing what to say. Finally, Willard broke the silence.

"Gee Jeff! This is so unfair. I mean, you don't deserve any of this. You're a good guy and you haven't done anything wrong. It wasn't your fault that some werewolf attacked you in the Yucatan. It wasn't your fault that you got afflicted with this curse. So why should this fall upon your shoulders? If only there was some way you could lift the curse."

There was another moment of silence, then suddenly Jeff lit up with an inspiration.

"Wait a minute! There's something in what you just said. Maybe there is a way to lift the curse."

"How, Jeff?"

"I don't know, but we're assuming that once a werewolf always a werewolf. And why do we think that? For the same reason that you believe in death by silver bullets. It's because of all those movies that we've seen. When you get right down to it, we really don't know anything about lycanthropy. Maybe there is some way to change me back to a normal human being."

"Okay, but how?"

"I don't know, but maybe there's someone out there who does."

"Well, who?"

"I don't know that either, but it seems to me—" Suddenly Jeff had another spark of insight. "Wait a minute! That fortune teller that you went to before. What was her name again?"

"Madam Esmeralda."

"Well, she told you how to solve my other problem, maybe she could help with this."

Willard shook his head.

"No, I don't think so. You see, she doesn't know anything about werewolves. It's her grandmother who is the expert. Esmeralda told me that she hates going to see the old woman. She said she'd never go out there again."

"Maybe if you offered her more money. Maybe that would change her mind. How much did you give her the last time?"

"Fifty dollars."

"Well, this time offer her two hundred."

Willard shook his head again.

"No, Mr. Cudmore would never go for that expense."

"Damn Cudmore!" said Jeff with unbridled vehemence. "I'll give you the money and we won't tell the old skinflint. I'll take the money out of my savings after work. I can have it for you first thing in the morning. Do you think you could go up to see Madam Esmeralda sometime tomorrow?"

"Yeah, I think so. I could go up there on my lunch hour." Willard hesitated for a minute then added, "I'll be glad to see Madam Esmeralda for you, but maybe she won't take the money. Or if she does, maybe her grandmother won't be able to help. In that case you'd be throwing your money away for nothing."

"Willard, right now losing two-hundred dollars is the very least of my problems. And if Esmeralda's grandmother can't help me, then at least I'll know what I'm up against–that there are no more options for me. Will you go see the woman for me, please?"

"Sure Jeff. I'll do my best for you."

"Thanks, Willard, you're a pal. I'll have the two hundred dollars for you tomorrow."

Early the next morning, Jeff went to his bank and withdrew two hundred dollars in cash from his savings account. He had the money ready when Willard arrived at the office. When he saw Willard come in, he walked over to the little man's cubbyhole and handed him a white envelope.

"Here it is, Willard," Jeff said in a low voice so no one else could hear. "In that envelope are ten twenties—two-hundred dollars."

Willard took the envelope and looked inside, then he put it in his pocket.

"Okay Jeff, I'll go up to Harlem and see Madam Esmeralda this afternoon."

That afternoon, Willard took the subway up to Harlem. He exited the station and he walked over to Lenox Avenue where Madam Esmeralda's studio was located. Once again, he climbed the rickety, dilapidated stairs to the second floor. He approached the door and was about to knock when he saw a sign tacked to the door. It said that Madam Esmeralda was away on vacation and wouldn't be back for fifteen days.

Willard stood there motionless, staring at the sign and thinking about the message. Fifteen days. Madam Esmeralda would be away all that time and out of reach. About two weeks before she got back and before he could consult with her. He and Jeff would have to wait two weeks for an answer to their problem. At that point they'd be fifteen days closer to the next full moon.

CHAPTER 26

Finally, Madam Esmeralda returned to her studio. It was now her first day back from her vacation. She had an enjoyable holiday, fifteen days visiting friends in Georgia, but now Esmeralda was home and she wanted to get back to telling fortunes so she could earn some money to pay for her vacation expenses. Suddenly, there was a knock on the door. When she heard that knock, she smiled to herself. It was only 9:30 a.m. and already her first paying customer had arrived.

She put on her robe, the turban and her jewelry, then she lumbered over to the door with a happy heart. Her joy, however, was short-lived, for when she flung open the door there was the pocket-sized figure of Willard Plotkin standing in the hallway.

"Ahhh Mouse! Not you again."

"Hello Madam Esmeralda, yes, it's me," said the diminutive Willard as he stood meekly before the gargantuan woman. "I have a problem that I need your help with."

She stood there for long seconds looking back at poor Willard debating with herself whether she wanted to talk with him or not. She really didn't like their first meeting, and she suspected that maybe this would be more of the same, so her first inclination was to shut the door in his face. However, as she stood looking back at Willard, she saw something in his mouse-like face that evoked a feeling of pity within her heart and she relented.

"All right," she sighed. "Come in and sit down. We'll talk, but somehow I have a feeling I'm gonna regret this."

Willard came in and sat at the round table. Madam Esmeralda opened her robe and threw off her turban as she made her way into the kitchen.

"I have a feeling I'm gonna need a beer for this conversation. You want one, Mouse?"

"No thank you, Madam Esmeralda, it's a little early in the day for me."

"Okay, suit yourself." With a can of brew in her hand she came back and plopped herself down in a chair opposite Willard. She placed the can of beer on the table before her and holding it with one hand, she pulled back the tab with her other. A spray of beer shot up like a geyser and hit the ceiling. She raised the can to her mouth and took a long swig.

"Okay, Mouse, tell me your problems. What is it this time, vampires?

"No, it's still the werewolf problem. You see my friend is in a bad way and we want to see if there's any way we can lift the curse and get him back to normal."

"Mouse," Esmeralda whined, "I told you I don't know anything about this werewolf hokum."

"Yes, I know. I remember you saying that, but I thought that maybe... well...that you could go out and pay a visit to your grandmother again and that maybe she—"

"Ah, come on, Mouse. I still haven't recovered from the last time that I went to see her. If you only knew what it was like to go out there and sit in her dusty house and eat her god-awful cookies and drink the slop that she calls tea, then you would never ask this of me."

Madam Esmeralda droned on about the suffering she experienced at her grandmother's. Willard continued to sit opposite her, maintaining his silence, not saying a word. Instead, he reached into his pocket and pulled out the white envelope that Jeff gave him. He extracted the fresh twenties and laid them in a row on the table before Madam Esmeralda. The big woman continued talking, but at the same time, she watched as he placed the crisp bills neatly and quietly on the table. Her speech became slower, quieter, and less deliberate until finally she'd shut her mouth completely by the time Willard had laid the last bill in place.

Willard sat back in silence and hoped that the money would do the talking needed to persuade the elephantine Esmeralda to make one more journey out to Grandma Poopootang's outpost.

For a long moment the mammoth woman didn't say anything; she continued to sit and stare at the two-hundred dollars on the table in front of her. As she looked down at the bills, she weighed in her mind the consequences of making another pilgrimage to see the venerable Grandma Poopootang. Was it worth, she wondered, contracting a chronic case of dyspepsia for two-hundred dollars? The money would sure be welcome, but would her innards ever be the same afterward? She bit her lip as she pondered her choices. She took another sip of beer and continued to debate both sides of the dilemma.

Finally, she said, "All right, Mouse, I'll do it. But this is absolutely, positively the last time that I go out there!"

Willard smiled. "Thank you, Madam Esmeralda, I can't tell you how much this means to us."

"Okay Mouse, but keep in mind that it's possible that Grandma Poopootang doesn't know anything more about this business. Or maybe she'll say there's no way to lift the curse of a werewolf. I mean, I don't know what she knows or doesn't know; I can't be sure of any tales the old woman has locked in the brain. Nevertheless, I get to keep the money no matter what she says, or doesn't say. You may be spending that money for nothing. You got that?"

"That's okay, Madam Esmeralda. You go out and talk to Grandma Poopootang. Then at least we will have tried, and my friend and I figure that it will be worth it."

"Okay Mouse, just so we understand each other. I'll go out to see the old lady tonight and I'll call you when I get back. You still at the same number?"

Willard nodded, rose and walked out. Madam Esmeralda didn't get up to walk him to the door, instead, she remained seated at the table looking at, studying, the two-hundred dollars laying before her. To her that was a great deal of money, but at the same time, she knew that she would have to earn it. That was going to be the hard part because she would have to go out and see Grandma Poopootang another time. When she thought about entering the old woman's dark, dusty house, and drinking her vile tea and eating her disgusting cookies, she shuddered, but a deal was a deal and Esmeralda was honorable enough to go through with it.

That evening Madam Esmeralda took the Seventh Avenue subway to the end of the line. She emerged from the bowels of the city onto the street and then walked the ten blocks to Grandma Poopootang's house. As she ambled slowly along those blocks, Esmeralda reflected upon the gloomy interior of Grandma Poopootang's house, the awful smells that permeated the atmosphere, and the woman's vile concoctions, and she dreaded the prospect ahead of her.

She thought to herself that she should have asked for two thousand dollars to make this trek. Better yet, she should have refused to go at all. But in a weak moment, she allowed the sight of the green money to sway her and she had, against her better judgment, agreed to come out here; and now she found herself lumbering along like an overstuffed hippopotamus to that solitary house in the middle of a deserted, rubble-strewn block wishing with every step that it would end quickly.

Eventually, Esmeralda found herself on the porch before the door to Poopootang's house. She manipulated the massive door knocker and sent a series of loud thuds reverberating through the interior of the house. Soon, Esmeralda heard the sound of shuffling feet from within and she knew that her antique grandmother was coming to the door. Again, the cacophony of chains and locks and tumblers and bolts signaled that the old woman was releasing the multitude of mechanical mechanisms that secured the front door.

The door creaked open and in the narrow gap there appeared the withered, old face of Grandma Poopootang.

"Ah ha! Look who has come to visit her old grandmother. It is my fine, fat, elephant girl, Esmeralda herself."

"Yes, Grandma Poopootang, it's me."

Poopootang opened the door wide.

"Well come in, come in. Come in and sit and talk with old Poopootang."

Esmeralda walked in and immediately her nostrils were attacked by the stench of some mixture that Poopootang had simmering in a cauldron on her stove in the kitchen, the room that smelled like a bovine burial ground. Poopootang led Esmeralda to her dimly-lit living room and bade the big, fat woman sit down. Esmeralda dropped her massive bulk into an immense overstuffed chair causing a humongous cloud of dust to shoot out from the upholstery and mingle with the dense stratosphere of the living room.

Esmeralda looked back at Poopootang and said a few words to initiate conversation, attempting to immediately declare the purpose of her visit while simultaneously hoping to distract her grandmother from bringing out the cookies and tea, but she was silenced by the old woman's upraised hand.

"Wait Esmeralda. Before we talk, you must have some of my tea and home-made cookies. You just sit there while I go to the kitchen and get a tray of food for you."

"Please Grandma Poopootang, I don't want to trouble you. I only came by to ask you—"

"Oh, it's no trouble, Esmeralda. I like to serve my guests. You know, I don't get many visitors."

Esmeralda winced. Small wonder. It was no surprise that visitors would shy away considering the typical fare that Poopootang always served as refreshment.

The old woman disappeared into the kitchen and in a short time came back carrying a tray with a bowl of steaming liquid and a plate of the sordid objects that she called her home-made cookies. She set the tray on the low table before Esmeralda's chair then stepped back to watch the fat lady partake of her offering. Under Poopootang's watchful eye, Esmeralda reached for the bowl and brought it to her lips. She closed her eyes so she wouldn't see what the repulsive liquid in the bowl looked like, and at the same time she held her breath lest she inhale and smell the putrid odor that rose from the foul concoction. Gamely she took a sip. She shuddered as she took her first swallow, for it tasted as if Grandma Poopootang had scooped the swill from a cesspool to make the stuff.

Then Esmeralda picked up a cookie, bit into it and masticated it, all the while trying desperately to keep her insides from retching. After taking a few sips of fetid tea and eating a whole ghastly cookie, Esmeralda composed herself and voiced the reason for her visit. She said that she wanted to know more about the curse of the werewolf, and if there were any way to lift it.

A slight smile crossed Poopootang's lips, but she said nothing. For the next couple of minutes, she was silent. Esmeralda waited, and the atmosphere turned very still. Then, after a few minutes of what seemed like suspended animation, the old woman came to life and began to speak. She started to talk about the creatures of the night who come alive in the light of the full moon. Esmeralda listened intently to the old woman's discourse, realizing at the same time that Poopootang's narrative would be a long one, and that she would have to drink more tea and eat at least three more disgusting cookies before Grandma Poopootang told her what she had come to hear.

CHAPTER 27

Willard was sitting alone in his tiny apartment watching television when the phone rang. He picked it up and murmured a greeting. A voice sounded which Willard immediately recognized as that of Madam Esmeralda.

"That you, Mouse?"

"Yes, Madam Esmeralda it's me, Willard. Did you get to go to Grandma Poopootang's house?"

"Yeah, I went and believe me when I tell you that it was an ordeal. I mean a real torment. My guts feel like they've been petrified. God, but I feel awful."

"I'm sorry, but did you find out anything about the curse of the werewolf? Did your Grandma Poopootang know anything about that?"

"Yeah, the old woman told me something, but I don't know how helpful it will be."

"What did she say?"

"She said that there may be a way to lift the curse, but she's not sure. She says legend has it that there is a flower that grows in the jungle and it, and it alone, has the power to lift the curse of the werewolf."

"A flower? That sounds kinda strange."

"Yeah, but that's what she said."

"What does this flower look like?"

"Well, that's a bit of a problem because she said she's never seen it, and she doesn't know anyone who has. She's just going by what the legends say. According to these legends, this strange flower only blooms in the light of the full moon. During the day it remains a closed bud and it looks much the same as any of the other plants around. At night, she says, when the light of the full moon hits it, then it opens up and becomes a beautiful flower that is totally different from anything that you've ever seen. She said that when it comes to bloom, it is so spectacular that you can't miss it."

"Well, what do you do when you find this flower? I mean how do you use it to rid yourself of the curse of the werewolf?"

"She didn't know that, but she suggests that you try rubbing it on yourself. If that doesn't work then maybe you should eat it. She said that she's not dead certain if it will work or not; she's just going by what the legends say."

There was a pause while Willard thought about all he was hearing. After a moment he asked, "Where do you find this flower? I mean where does it grow?"

"Poopootang didn't know that either, but she thinks it probably grows in the territory where the werewolves run. She suggests that your friend go back to the place where he was first attacked by the werewolf and look there."

There was a long pause during which neither Willard nor Esmeralda spoke. Finally, the fat woman broke the silence.

"Look Mouse, I know this isn't much help, but it's all that Poopootang seemed to know."

"No, Madam Esmeralda, this has been very helpful. At least now we have something to look for and a place to look for an answer and we have some hope. That's more than we had before. Thank you."

"You're welcome, Mouse. I hope this works because if it doesn't, don't ask me to go back to Poopootang's house again—at least not for another year. My guts just couldn't take it."

"Don't worry, Madam Esmeralda, if this doesn't work then I have a feeling that we'll have reached the end of the line and we won't be bothering you anymore. Thank you for all your help."

"Again, you're welcome Mouse. And good luck. I have a feeling you're gonna need it."

The next day, Willard went to see Jeff and tell him all he'd learned from Madam Esmeralda. Jeff listened to everything Willard had to tell him without saying a word. Even after Willard finished, Jeff remained silent, lost in thought.

Willard waited for him to say something but there was nothing; finally, he asked, "Jeff, what are you going to do now?"

"Well, it seems like the only thing I can do is go back to the Yucatan and look for that flower. Right now, that's the only hope I've got."

"Do you think you'll be able to find it?"

Jeff shrugged. "I have no idea; but I've got to try. After all, I don't have any options left at this point."

Willard nodded in agreement. "When do you think you'll be going?"

"As soon as I can book a flight. The full moon is only a week away, so I don't have much time to waste."

Willard nodded again and they both sat there in mutual silence for another minute, then Jeff looked up at Willard and asked a question.

"Willard, I want to ask a favor of you. I know it's a big favor that I'm asking, but it would mean a lot to me if you would grant it."

"Sure, Jeff. I'll try if I can."

"I want you to come with me to the Yucatan. As I said, I know it's a lot to ask, but I'd really like you to come with me."

Willard gulped at this unexpected request.

"Why Jeff? I mean, I'm no Tarzan. What can I do?"

"Willard, I'm not sure what will happen or what I'm going to find. Maybe I won't even come back. If not, I'd like to have someone along, someone who can come back to New York and explain what happened to me. Will you come along, if only for moral support?"

"Well gee, Jeff, surely there must be someone else, a close friend or relative, who would be better than me at helping you."

Jeff thought about that for a minute, then shook his head.

"Nope. The truth is, I can't think of anyone else who could help me. I know that we're not the closest of friends. We barely know each other outside of the office…but, well…I feel that after all that's happened, somehow there is a bond between us. After all, you've been in on my werewolf life almost from the beginning. You understand my problem like no one else. You're the only one I really can trust. Please say you'll come."

Willard thought about the request. For almost all of his life, Willard's life had been calm, safe and simple. He'd only thought of himself as a small, timid man—certainly not an adventurer—and the thought of going to the jungles of the faraway Yucatan, into the wilds where the beast of the night roams, unnerved him.

Born and raised in New York City, he'd never gone beyond its borders, never gone hiking in the woods, nor done anything even remotely daring or risky. Now suddenly, it was as if he was being asked to do something that required the courage of a tiger, and poor, little Willard, the mouse-man that he was, didn't know if he had it in him.

As he thought about going with Jeff to the far reaches of civilization, he knew that it was the last thing he wanted to do, and all of him wanted to say no; but when he looked back at Jeff's face, he saw something that approached desperation in the man's eyes. That faint look, kindled with a vague note of compassion deep within his soul, motivated Willard and the little man relented.

"Okay, I'll go with you if you want me to. What should I tell Mr. Cudmore?"

"Tell him that you have to take time off to see a sick friend. Don't worry about the expenses, I'll make the reservations and take care of everything.

161

I'll pay for everything. None of this will cost you a dime. Thanks, Willard, you're a true friend. I really mean that."

Willard nodded. He knew that he had just agreed to help out his friend, but at the same time, he was nervous about what he was about to get into. Yet, he realized that he had just agreed to go and, now, like it or not, Willard was going to be in this adventure to the bitter end.

The next morning, Jeff announced that all the plane and hotel reservations were in place and they would depart on the following day. Willard tried to assume a façade of bravado, a cavalier, self-assured posture, but inside he was a restless bundle of apprehension. He knew that he was being called up to be stalwart and brave, but never in his life had Willard ever been any of those things. What's more, Willard had never been outside of the United States before, and the thought occurred to him that going to the dense faraway jungles to face unknown monsters while searching for a mythical, mysterious flower in the dark of the night was a hell of a place to begin.

CHAPTER 28

The next day, Jeff and Willard took the morning plane to Cozumel. They flew south and arrived at the airport in Cozumel later that same day. They ended up in a modest, no-frills hotel. The full moon was only three nights away, but they decided that they would spend the first night in Cozumel then take the ferry to the mainland the following day.

After a night in Cozumel, they boarded the ferry to the mainland. During the ride across the water, neither man offered much in the way of conversation. Both seemed to be apprehensive and somehow this did not seem like the time for small talk.

From time to time, however, Willard glanced at his companion, and noted that by all outward appearances, Jeff was calm and impassive. Willard tried to adopt a similar composure, but inside he was starting to get nervous. He knew that every moment brought them closer to the jungle, the territory where the mysterious creatures of the night dwelled and his mind was churning over the many dangers that they could face.

What would happen when they got there? What would they find? Suppose they ran into that very same creature that ravaged Jeff? Jeff could afford to be calm and even relaxed because he was one of them. But what about little Willard? Suppose the creature attacked, bit him and made him into a werewolf? Wouldn't that be a shocking combination: Willard, a timid mouse-man by day and a vicious wolfman by night.

When the boat reached the port and docked, all the passengers disembarked. Jeff led Willard to the bus stop and the two men boarded an old, rickety bus. Soon they were rattling and bouncing along a back road that took them through jungles, farmland, small villages, and past native dwellings.

Willard sat by the window and gazed out at the passing scenery. He had never seen anything like this—except in books and movies. Now, however, he was actually traveling through forests, jungles, and towns, seeing people and sights that were totally new to the small world that he'd always known. It all seemed fascinating and exotic to him, yet at the same time, he could not relax and enjoy himself, because he knew that with each passing mile they were getting closer to their final destination, the forbidden jungle, the land where the werewolf, the creature of the night, roamed in the light of the full moon.

Finally, the bus pulled into a small town, and Jeff announced that this was it, their final destination. They got off the bus and made their way to the town's only hotel just a small distance away.

When they entered and walked up to the weathered front desk, the clerk looked up and greeted them. Willard noticed that the man seemed a little curious and maybe even nervous, at the sudden arrival of his new guests. Perhaps, thought Willard, it was because the man had recognized Jeff and remembered him from the time before. Maybe he knew that Jeff had been bitten by the jungle creature and suspected that Willard might be one himself. Maybe now he was wondering why this American had returned. Whatever his thoughts, he kept them to himself as he pushed the register book forward and handed Jeff a pen.

Both Jeff and Willard signed the register, took their room keys and climbed the stairs to the second floor where they found that their rooms were directly across the hall from each other. Jeff went into his room and Willard opened the door and entered his.

Willard found that it was small, not opulent or luxurious, but clean and neat. There was a sink, but no bathroom. He imagined that the toilet and shower, if they existed, would be down the hall. Well, Jeff could explain that later; for now, Willard wanted to just settle in and maybe lie down and try to relax. He dropped his bag on a chair and stretched out on the bed, but found that he was so tense and apprehensive and he just couldn't relax.

This wasn't a vacation; they were here for a somber purpose and that thought weighed heavily upon Willard. He rose from the bed, and walked to the window. He was surprised to see that there were bars on the window. He looked past them and out at the landscape. There, not too far off, were the mountains. Jeff had told him that his encounter with the werewolf had happened on a mountaintop. No doubt they would be making a trek up one of those mountains very soon. And what would they find when they got there?

At that moment there was a knock on the door. It was Jeff. He came to suggest that they go for lunch. Willard readily agreed and the two left the hotel for the cantina.

The cantina was a quiet place with about a half-dozen empty tables. Jeff and Willard seated themselves at one of the center tables and when the waiter came over they ordered some food and two beers. They sat there and ate without saying much. As they were just about finished, a man walked into the cantina and approached their table. Jeff looked up.

"Hello Miguel," he said, "it's good to see you again."

Miguel nodded. "I heard that you had arrived in town, Señor. I thought that I would come and see you."

"I'm glad you did. It saves me the trouble of finding you. I need your help. Sit down and I'll tell you about it." Miguel took up a chair opposite Jeff. "Would you like a beer?"

Miguel nodded. When the beer arrived, Miguel took a swig, Jeff proceeded to explain the reason why he and Willard had come back to the Yucatan. He told Miguel about the mysterious flower and the reason that he had to find it. Miguel listened to all of this without saying a word. He just listened and sipped his beer.

Jeff concluded: "Miguel, I must find this flower, and I need you to take me back up the mountain to the same place that we went before."

"Señor, what you say is loco. I have been through the jungle many times and I have never seen this flower that you talk about. I do not think that there is such a flower. You are wasting your time."

"Maybe, but then you've never been in the jungle when the full moon is up. So, if the flower does, in fact exist, there is no way that you could have seen it. But let's not argue about this. The point is that I need to go back up the mountain and I need you to guide me. Will you do it?"

Miguel took another swig of beer and then sat and thought about what Jeff was asking him to do. After a minute of contemplation, he answered, "All right, Señor, I will take you back to the same place that I took you before; but I will not stay with you after the sun goes down. What you want to do is your business, but when night falls and the moon comes up, I will be back in my own home behind a locked door."

"Agreed," said Jeff.

Now during this entire exchange, Willard just sat there looking from Jeff to Miguel and back again. Both men talked back and forth between each other, virtually ignoring Willard. As he sat there listening, Willard understood that when the full moon rose in the sky, Miguel would be safe at home and Jeff would remain in the jungle, but where would he, little insignificant Willard, be at that time? Would he be back in his hotel room or would he be in the jungle with Jeff? That thought worried Willard but neither Jeff nor Miguel seemed to have entertained that bit of info and somehow, he felt asking would display cowardice. He hoped that he would know what to do when the time came.

The next morning, the three men met outside the hotel and started their trek up the mountain. Miguel led the way with Jeff following and Willard bringing up the rear. Willard had short legs and a slow gait, but fortunately, Miguel paused occasionally so Willard was able to keep up.

During all this time, whether walking through the jungle, following the path up the mountain, or stopping to take a break, no one said a word. It was as if the gravity of their mission had shorted out any impulse to make idle conversation. Willard racked his brain for a whimsical remark or lighthearted joke to introduce a note of levity and lighten up the mood. But alas, it was not to be, and the three continued trekking up the mountain in grave silence.

At last, they reached the clearing at the summit of the mountain. Miguel walked to the center of the clearing, turned and announced to his companions, "Señors, we are here."

Jeff nodded and looked around. "Yep, this is the place all right. It's just as I remember it. Well, let's have a bite to eat before we start looking around."

The trio sat down, opened up their backpacks, pulled out their food, and commenced eating lunch. As they sat eating in silence, Willard looked around taking in the magnificence of their surroundings. In all his sheltered life, he had never seen anything quite like this before. The jungle, the exotic vegetation, the mountains, the azure sky—the whole panorama was awesome, and Willard wished he could take time out, relax and just enjoy the beauty of this spot. Unfortunately, just as Willard was starting to do that, Jeff announced that they should begin searching for the object of their quest, the elusive flower that had the power to lift the curse of lycanthropy.

The three men got up and began to explore the clearing, peering behind the bushes and shrubs for anything that might possibly be an unusual, out-of-the-ordinary, specimen of plant life. Then they widened their search pattern by walking into adjacent jungle areas.

Jeff and Miguel plunged into the bush casually, but Willard was more apprehensive. As he stepped into the high grass and dense bush, he stepped cautiously because he feared that the vegetation could be concealing some serpent or wild animal that would leap out without warning and bite him. He looked very carefully before he moved and then stepped gingerly so that he wouldn't unexpectedly encounter any snakes or carnivores.

After almost two hours of searching, Miguel came back to the center of the clearing. As soon as Jeff came out of the bush Miguel confronted him.

"Señor, we have looked all around us and we have found nothing. I do not believe that this flower you seek exists."

"You may be right, Miguel; but we can't be sure of that until we see what happens when the full moon comes out. That is the time that the flower is supposed to show itself. Only when that happens will we know for sure."

"Señor, we had agreed—"

Jeff cut him off. "I know. You are to go back and be safe at home before the moon comes up. Well, it's getting late. I guess you had better start back now."

Jeff turned to Willard. "Willard, you had better go back with Miguel. I'm not going back, not just yet anyway. I will stay up here by myself and watch the moon come up."

"Jeff, are you sure? If you want, I'll—"

"No Willard, thank you for the offer, but it's better that you should return. Go back with Miguel."

"Okay Jeff."

Inwardly, Willard breathed a silent sigh of relief. Staying up on the mountaintop in the middle of the night with the full moon high in the sky and strange beasts running wild in the jungle was the very last thing that he wanted to do, but he never mentioned his uneasiness lest he appear cowardly. Now, comforted by the knowledge that he was returning to the security of the village hotel, he felt as if a great burden was lifted from his heart. He picked up his backpack and joined Miguel. The two walked to the edge of the clearing, but just before they started on the path at the edge of the jungle, Willard turned one last time to look back. Jeff was standing in the middle of the clearing. He looked back at Willard, smiled, and gave a small wave. Willard smiled faintly and waved, at the same time wondering if he would ever see his friend again.

CHAPTER 29

Now with Willard and Miguel gone, Jeff was alone in the clearing on the mountaintop and he felt as if the scenes of a year ago were coming back to him and replaying themselves like a familiar movie. He walked about the clearing slowly, looking all around, and as he did this, he had the uncanny feeling that he was reliving the exact memory of his previous time on this very spot—only now there was one significant difference. This time he wasn't there for sightseeing, this time he was seeking a mysterious magical flower that might help him return to normality.

Unfortunately, there was no sign of it. Soon, the sun made its descent and the sky turned from blue, to red-orange then to gray, and finally to dense, inky black, and Jeff was surrounded by opaque darkness. He looked around, but couldn't see much of anything. Well, maybe when the moon came up, it would provide enough light to see by. Maybe when the moon came up, that elusive flower would blossom and reveal itself—that is, if it existed at all. Until the moon rose, however, there was nothing to do but wait and hope. Jeff let out a deep sigh, then found a comfortable rock, sat down and waited.

The various hidden beings—those insects and birds and reptiles of the night that make their presence known by their medley of chirps, squeaks, croaks, and other various vocalizations began their symphony and filled the night with sound. For many long moments, Jeff sat there in the darkness with only the sounds of the jungle providing dimension to the black void in which he was sitting. Presently the moon rose and bathed the jungle with a surreal light that transformed the plants and trees into ghostly images.

Jeff got up and walked to the middle of the clearing. He turned about, scanning the ground and the grass, plants and bushes for some trace of that strange and shadowy flower that he'd come over two thousand miles to find, but there was no sign of it. He looked about, turning slowly in a complete circle while, all the time peering into the vegetation for some sign of a stalk or bush…something that was different than the rest. But still, there was nothing.

Jeff was starting to get anxious. He knew that soon the moon would rise to its full height and take its effect on his body and then he would change into a werewolf. That time was not long in coming, and he knew that he had to find that flower before that horrible change happened. Just when he began to think all was lost, that the enchanted flower was just a myth and didn't really exist, just when Jeff had almost convinced himself that he had come all this way for nothing, he saw something out of the corner of his eye.

He turned and looked, and that is when he saw it. There on the edge of the clearing was a large bud that apparently had just opened. Jeff walked over to it and saw that large white petals were bursting forth from the open bud. In less than a minute, the petals spread to form a beautiful flower that seemed to glow with iridescence in the light of the full moon. As he looked down at the magnificent blossom, Jeff realized that he was looking at a flower unlike any that he had ever seen in his life. It was beautiful, and he was sure that this strange, exotic flower was the one for which he'd so eagerly sought. Jeff looked down at the remarkable flower with its wide, radiant petals and it was like looking at an organic jewel. He was mesmerized by its strange beauty. At that moment he truly believed that this exotic blossom really did have the power to lift the curse of the beast within him.

He was about to reach down and pluck it from its stem when he paused for a moment to listen. Up till now, he'd been so absorbed in searching for the elusive flora that he failed to notice that the many sounds in the bush had faded and now silence enveloped the jungle. He stood there listening, but there was nothing to hear. All was quiet, all was still. The little nocturnal creatures of the jungle had ceased making their peculiar music and Jeff knew what that meant, because he'd experienced this eerie silence before.

He stood there, fixed to the spot, continuing to listen, and he waited. He waited for the sound that he knew must follow. Soon he heard it. It was the rustle of the leaves, the sound of something moving in the bush. It was faint at first, then grew progressively louder. Something was moving in the jungle, and it was coming closer.

Then it was quiet again. Jeff continued to stand very still with his ears tuned to his surroundings. Then he heard a low growl, and when Jeff turned and looked behind him, he saw two red eyes glowing in the darkness; and Jeff knew that the jungle creature of the night had found him again.

Willard woke up the next morning with the sun streaming in his window. He must have been very tired the night before, because he dropped off to sleep the moment his head hit the pillow and, shockingly, he had slept soundly through the night. Now, he woke up feeling sudden terror for Jeff. He rolled over to the bedside table where his wristwatch lay and he looked at the dial. It was 9:30.

He lay back and looked up at the ceiling. He thought back to the climb of the previous day. He remembered that he'd left Jeff on the mountaintop and returned with Miguel to the village. They'd arrived at the village before sunset. Willard remembered that later he went to the cantina for supper, had little appetite, and quickly returned to his room where he got into bed. He'd tried to read but was so tired that he kept nodding off. Finally, he turned out the light to go to sleep. That was about 10:30. Ten-thirty. That meant that he had slept for about eleven hours? He must have been incredibly tired to sleep that long.

Well, now it was the morning of the following day. Willard rolled out of bed, grabbed his towel and walked down the hall to the shower room. It wasn't until he returned to his room and started to get dressed that Willard thought about Jeff. What had happened to Jeff?

Still in his underwear he hurried across the hall and knocked on Jeff's door. No answer. Cautiously, Willard tried the knob and found that the door wasn't locked. He opened it a crack and called Jeff's name, but still there was no answer. Slowly and quietly, he pushed the door back and peered inside. He saw that the bed was still made up and everything was in the same place as the previous day. It looked as if Jeff hadn't come down from the mountain yet. Willard pulled the door shut and remained standing there in the hall thinking about what he should do next.

He decided that all he could do was wait for Jeff to come back. Willard dressed and went to the cantina for breakfast. After eating, he returned to the hotel to peek into Jeff's room again, but the result was the same: Jeff still had not returned.

Willard was at a loss. After carefully considering his situation, he decided that his only option was to hang around town waiting and hoping that Jeff would come back soon. So, Willard spent the day walking around the village, eating at the cantina and sitting in his room reading. Occasionally, he'd hurry to Jeff's room to see if his friend had returned, but the result was always the same: the room was empty and there was no sign of Jeff.

That night, Willard seemed to wake coated in perspiration every hour or so. His thoughts were troubled by what he should do the following day. He knew that he had only one more day to spend in the village because he was scheduled to fly back to New York the following afternoon. Then he would have to take a bus to the ferry, and go from there to Cozumel to catch his plane. He didn't want to miss that plane, and yet he didn't want to leave the Yucatan without finding out what happened to Jeff.

At one point in the middle of the night, he thought that he heard the howl of wolves somewhere off in the distance, but he wasn't sure if it was a dream or actual reality. Finally, in the wee hours of the morning Willard fell into a sound sleep and he didn't hear anything more.

It was late the next morning when Willard woke up. He immediately jumped from the bed, showered, then dressed and went out to the cantina for breakfast. As he ate, he tried to formulate some sort of game plan, and by the time he finished his meal, he'd put together a rough strategy in his mind. He left the cantina and went through the village for Miguel. This was a small village and Miguel was well-known to all, so Willard had no trouble finding the guide.

When the two met, Willard immediately told Miguel that Jeff had not returned from the jungles.

"That is not surprising, Señor. After all, the jungle is a very dangerous place at night."

"I know that, but I have to find him. I want you to take me back up the mountain, to the place where we left him."

"That will do no good. You will not find him there."

"You may be right, but I have to try. I can't go back to New York without at least trying to find him this one time. Then, at least I will know in my own mind that I did my best. Will you take me up there?"

Miguel shrugged. "All right, Señor, I will take you back to the mountain, but we must return before dark."

"Agreed!" said Willard.

So, the two men arranged to get food from the cantina and then began their trek through the jungles and back up the mountain. After a long, tiring walk, they reached the clearing on top of the mountain. When they got there, Willard walked into the center of the clearing and looked all around, but there was nothing. There was absolutely no sign of Jeff.

Miguel had seated himself on a rock. "I told you, Señor, that there would be nothing to find here. Your friend is gone and you will not find him."

"Maybe, but let me look around some. There may be some sign."

"As you wish. Whatever pleases you."

So, Willard walked about the clearing and ventured into the bush as far as he dared, but all to no avail. He searched as hard as he could, but there was no sign of Jeff.

After about two hours, Miguel announced, "Señor, it is getting late. We must start back now if we are to get to the village before dark."

Willard nodded and walked over to pick up his backpack. Then the two men walked out of the clearing and made their way down the mountain.

It was still light when they returned to the village. Willard went back to his hotel to clean up after his dusty, sweaty trek, then he tried Jeff's door again. The result was the same: Jeff still had not returned. By now Willard was convinced that his worst fears had been realized—that Jeff had most likely been attacked by the night beast and had probably been carried off into the jungle. In all likelihood he was dead and Willard would have to return to New York without him. Crestfallen, Willard went to the cantina for supper.

The sun was just starting to drop when Willard emerged from the cantina, and rather than go back to his hotel where he would have nothing to do, he decided to sit outside while it was still light and maybe watch the sunset. That would certainly be better than staring at the four blank walls in his hotel room, and maybe being outside for a while would take his mind off his troubles.

Willard found a roughhewn bench beneath a big tree and he sat down. For a long while he just sat there under the tree, watching the sunset and also looking around him at the buildings and the few people still outside. Then he started to ponder his situation, and think about what his next move should be, but try as he might, he had no idea what he should do.

Willard realized that in all his life, he had never been in a situation like this. Always, for as long as he could remember, there had always been someone in his life to tell him what to do, to guide and direct him and often even order him to action. First, it was his mother and father, then his teachers, his older sisters, then his supervisors at jobs, finally it was Damon Cudmore. And Willard recalled that he had always followed these authoritarian figures almost without question. He did that because it's what he had been trained to do from the very beginning of his life.

Now, however, here he was, over two-thousand miles from home, in a strange and unfamiliar country, in the middle of a small village surrounded by people he didn't know, and he was alone. There was no one within thousands of miles that he could turn to for advice or direction. There was no one to tell him what to do.

Then suddenly, as he was sitting there, slowing sinking into despair, he heard a voice call out his name. Startled, Willard turned around and saw his friend, Jeff Foxlove standing less than ten feet away.

CHAPTER 30

Willard was in shock by the sudden appearance of his friend. Even though Jeff was standing there in plain sight, Willard still couldn't believe his senses. Up till that moment, he'd convinced himself that Jeff was dead and gone and would never be seen again. Now, however, there, standing less than ten feet away, was the living, breathing figure of Jeff. Willard sat still for a long minute, completely dumbfounded, unsure if he was looking at a live person or merely some sort of apparition. Slowly and cautiously he rose and walked toward his friend.

"Jeff," he said, "is it really you? You're still alive?"

Jeff smiled. "Yes, Willard, it's me. I'm here, and I'm very much alive."

"Oh, Jeff! I thought that you were dead. If you only knew how worried I was."

"I'm sorry. I suppose I should have come back sooner, but it was kind of difficult."

"Did you find the flower?"

"Yes, Willard, I found the flower."

"Did it work? Did it cure you?"

"I don't know. I never got to try it."

"I don't understand. I mean if you found the flower, why didn't you try it? What happened? What did you do with it?"

"I didn't do anything with it." Jeff could see the look of puzzlement on Willard's face. "Look, this is going to take some explaining on my part. Let's go to the bench under that tree and sit down. Then I'll tell you the whole story."

So, the pair walked over to the bench and sat down. Jeff began his tale.

"When you and Miguel left me alone on the mountain, I looked for that mysterious flower. At first, I couldn't find it, but then when the full moon rose, there it was. And when it opened up and blossomed I knew it was the flower I searched for because it was blooming at night and was unlike any that I'd ever seen before. I was ready to reach down and pluck it from its stem, but for a moment I hesitated."

"Why?"

"Well, I heard something in the bushes behind me. I turned and sure enough, there she was."

"She?"

"Yes, Willard. It was the other werewolf, the same one who attacked me a year ago when I was at that very place. I didn't realize it at the time, but that werewolf was a female. And when she attacked me, she wasn't trying to kill me. No, she only wanted to bite me so I would turn into a beast like her, and be her mate."

"Jeff, that's…that's…well, that's beyond crazy. I mean it's unbelievable."

"Yeah! I know it is, but it's true nevertheless. She wanted me for her mate. The only problem was, she couldn't know that I was from another country, far away. She couldn't know that I would leave this place and go back to New York. But I suppose she must have known that even if I did leave, someday I might return. After all, where else could I live but here, in the land of the creature of the night, the werewolf?"

Jeff paused for a minute to see if Willard was absorbing all he was saying. Willard had been listening with wide-eyed intensity to Jeff's narrative, but at the same time, he couldn't quite believe his ears because the whole tale sounded weird and surreal. He waited for Jeff to continue.

When he didn't, Willard finally asked, "Well, what happened then? You two were on the mountain together under the full moon, so what did you do?"

"Well, for those first few minutes, nothing. We just stood there looking at each other. You see, she was in her full wolf form and I was still a human. But then the light of the full moon started to affect me and I began to change from man to beast. In a few minutes there we were, both werewolves together. And that was the glorious part."

"Glorious? It sounds terrible to me. What was so glorious about it?"

"Well, at that point, it was as if we'd become one. I mean we were still two separate animals in two bodies, but at the same time, we were one kindred spirit, one mingled soul. It was as if we had this common life-force that we both shared. I tell you it was truly sublime because I felt a spiritual attachment to her. The sensation was explosive, unlike anything that I had ever experienced before."

Willard shook his head, unable to fully understand what Jeff was talking about, yet still wanting to hear all the details of this incredible story.

"What happened then?"

"Then we went into the jungle together and together we ran wild as a pair, hunting and moving side by side, as two beings separate in body, but one in mind and spirit. For me it was unbelievable, because with her at my side I suddenly felt a sense of freedom and power that I'd never experienced in all my life.

"At the same time, I felt that I was in touch with a part of myself that had been hidden for so long but yearning to be free. It was as if I could now be all of me, with all of my parts and impulses out and fully functioning."

Willard stared at Jeff, not quite sure what all this meant.

"How long did all of this last?"

"For almost the whole night. When the night was just about spent, and when we could see that dawn was about to break, we went back to her place—she has a small home on the other side of the mountains. We went inside, lay down and fell asleep together. The next day, when I awoke, we were back to our human forms. She was still asleep, resting in my arms, and when I looked at her, I saw that she was the most beautiful woman I had ever seen in my entire life."

"So now that the sun was up and you were both human again, then what? I mean how did you spend the day? What did you do?"

Jeff shrugged. "Not much. Reena—that's her name–has a small farm. I helped her work it a bit. And that was wonderful too, because even as humans we still had that same, unspoken spiritual bond between us. Reena doesn't speak much English, but that doesn't matter, because we seem to be able to communicate on a higher plane. We seemed to know what the other is thinking and feeling without the use of words. I tell you, Willard, that I've never met anyone to whom I've ever felt so close in all my life.

"Besides all of that, there was another feeling. When I had regained my human form, I felt as if I had been cleansed. I realized that I'd gotten in touch with another part of myself...I guess you could call it my animal part...anyway, now that I'd explored that hidden side of me, I felt... well...I guess you could say I felt like a whole new man."

"All that is well and good," said Willard. "I mean, I'm glad you found a companion and had a good time and got in touch with all your parts, but now what? Don't forget that our plane for New York leaves tomorrow. In the meantime, do you think that maybe you should find that flower and see if you can use it to lift the werewolf curse so you'll be all right when you go back?"

There was a long pause.

Jeff looked hard at Willard, then finally said, "I won't need the flower, because I'm not going back to New York."

Willard looked back at Jeff in disbelief. Had he heard that correctly?

"What do you mean? You have to go back to New York. That's where you live and work. That's where your life is."

"Not anymore. For the past two days, I've been thinking this over very carefully and I've decided that this is the place for me. I want to stay and live here with Reena."

"But Jeff," exclaimed Willard, "this is the jungle out here. I mean it's wild and uncivilized, and you're not an animal."

"I'm not? Maybe not, and then again maybe I am. I think that maybe we're all animals to some degree. Only the civilized world that we live in makes us suppress that side of us. Although in some people like Damon Cudmore, it's not very far below the surface.

"As for jungles, well, I know that it's a tired cliché to say that New York is a jungle, but it is. When I look back over these past seven months, I see all the things that Cudmore made me do, things that I had to do to fit into Madison Avenue and the rest of New York. When I think about that, I truly believe that the buildings and cars and buses, restaurants and stores and designer clothing—everything that we call civilization is just a veneer and that deep down, New York is just as wild and savage as it is here."

"Jeff, you're only saying that because you're remembering your experience back there as a werewolf. Use the flower to change yourself and then come back. Things will be different once you become completely human again. New York will seem friendlier then."

Jeff shook his head. "No Willard. You're forgetting something."

"What?"

"You're forgetting about Reena. I told you that I don't want to leave her."

"Couldn't you take her back with you?"

"No, she was born and raised here. This is the only country and the only environment that she's known. She could never adjust to life in New York."

"You can't be sure of that, Jeff. I mean, with your help she would probably adjust and who knows, she might actually get to like the big city."

"Maybe, although I doubt it. I think that she'd be miserable. Anyway, there's another, stronger reason that she can't go to New York."

"What's that?"

"You're forgetting that she's a werewolf."

"Yeah, but she doesn't have to be. You can use the magic flower to transform her. Then she'd be human like the rest of us and she wouldn't have to worry about the full moon. I'll bet that she'd like that."

Jeff shook his head. "No, it won't work. You see, she's different than me. She didn't become a werewolf from a bite. She was born a werewolf. Both of her parents were werewolves. It's in her blood, in her genes. She told me that the flower won't work for her. It will for me, but not for her.

"If I take her back to the city with me, then every time the full moon came up, she would turn into a wolf and go out to kill someone. Eventually, the police would hunt her down and murder her. No, this is the only place where she can live and be free. Here, when the full moon comes up and transforms her, she can roam the jungle and kill other animals. The people around here know to stay indoors at night. They have bars on their windows. So, they are safe and no one ever gets hurt. This is the only place for her."

"I see."

Willard was crestfallen. He saw that Jeff had made up his mind and was determined to stay in this place. At the same time, he understood that Jeff was right; if he wanted to stay with his beloved Reena, then this was the only place for him. There seemed to be nothing more to say. Willard would have to return to New York by himself and that depressed him. He sat there in silence looking down at the ground. Jeff smiled and patted him on the shoulder.

"Cheer up, little buddy. It's not so bad. In fact, I really like it out here. When you meet Reena, you'll understand everything. Besides, from now on, I won't have to work with Damon Cudmore in his sleaze-ball world."

"Yeah, but I'm going to miss you, Jeff. You were the only friend I had up at the agency."

"I know. I feel the same about you; but I guess life goes on and we have to move with it. You'll adjust, Willard. Somehow, you'll find a way, because, believe it or not, you really are a very resourceful guy. You just haven't had the chance to prove yourself. You can be extremely strong when you want to be."

Willard looked at Jeff and tried to smile, but it was a weak smile because he was still sad at the prospect of losing his friend and inwardly, in spite of what Jeff had said about him, he had doubts as to his own abilities.

"Well, Willard, it's getting late and I want to get back to Reena. But I'll return in the morning and see you before you get on the bus."

Jeff stood and walked away. Willard sat there for a few more minutes before he went back to the hotel all by himself. He felt very lost and was sad at the prospect of going home alone.

CHAPTER 31

The next morning Willard got up, showered and dressed. Then he packed his small suitcase and checked out of the hotel. When Willard emerged from the hotel into the open air, he looked around to see if maybe Jeff was somewhere around waiting for him, but he wasn't. Willard went to the cantina and ate breakfast, then went to the bus stop.

Willard sat there and waited for the bus to arrive and for Jeff to show up for their final goodbye, but a full hour passed and there was no sign of either. As he sat there waiting for one or both to appear. What would he do if the bus pulled in before Jeff came? Should he get on the bus and leave without saying goodbye this one last time to Jeff? Or should he let the bus go and chance missing the ferry and his plane? It was a quandary for poor Willard and he hated being in quandaries. He hated having to make decisions by himself. Fortunately, he didn't have to make that decision, for when he looked up and around, he saw Jeff walking toward him.

Jeff was not alone; there was a woman walking beside him. Willard assumed that this was the wolf-woman of the jungle, the mysterious Reena. As the two came closer, Willard could see what Jeff had said was true—this woman was truly beautiful. In fact, she was the most beautiful woman he'd ever laid eyes on.

She wore a thin white dress that clung to her and revealed her trim, curvy, and slightly muscular figure. She walked with ease, flowing from step to step with the graceful strides of a lithe feline. As they got closer, Willard could see that there wasn't an ounce of fat on her body. Her hair was straight and black and flowed down to her shoulders framing her beautiful face.

They came up to Willard and Jeff said, "Willard, I'd like you to meet my companion, Reena."

Willard looked up to Reena. It seemed that she was even more beautiful close up. And now, at close range, he saw how tall she was. She was a full head taller than he. She had a svelte, muscular figure. As he looked up to her face, Willard saw that she had a pair of intense, exotic, wide, black eyes. Reena didn't say anything but she extended her hand and smiled down at Willard. When her lips parted, Willard could see that her two front canines were long and pointed, giving her mouth the hint of the savage, lupine animal that lay hidden beneath the human figure of graceful femininity.

Willard mumbled something to the effect that he was pleased to meet her. He wanted to say something more, but he felt a little awkward standing before such a beautiful, sensuous woman. Her magnetic presence seemed to stupefy him and he couldn't make either his brain or his tongue function properly. So, he just stood there, motionless, tongue-tied and feeling self-conscious. Neither Jeff nor Reena spoke either, but as far as Willard could tell neither seemed the least bit uncomfortable.

At that moment the bus suddenly appeared as if from nowhere, and it pulled up to the stop where the three were waiting. The door opened and the driver stepped out and beckoned the waiting passengers to enter his dilapidated vehicle. It was time to board, but Willard found himself unable to move. He continued standing there looking at Jeff and his beautiful feral-human companion.

Jeff finally spoke up. "Well, Willard, I guess this is goodbye."

Willard nodded. His moment of departure had arrived and he knew he'd have to get on board or he'd be left behind; but he continued to stand there waiting, hoping that maybe Jeff would change his mind and come with him. Jeff, however, remained in place, and Willard knew intuitively that it was not to be.

"Willard, when you get back, I'd like you to call my girlfriend—my ex-girlfriend now—and tell her that I'm not coming back to New York. Here, I've written her name and number down on this piece of paper."

Willard took the paper and looked at it. "What should I tell her when she asks why you're not coming back?"

Jeff thought about it for a moment, then said, "Tell her that I followed the yellow brick road and that I'm now in the magical land of Oz."

"Huh? Do you think she'll understand that?"

Jeff shook his head. "No, but then she doesn't understand anything else in life, so it doesn't really matter. All she has to understand is that I'm not ever coming back to New York."

There was another long moment of silence while Willard tried to think of something to say, something to prolong the moment. Something to delay the inevitable departure.

"What should I tell Mr. Cudmore?"

"Tell him that I said to go to Hell. I'm sure he'll understand that."

Willard nodded. At that moment the bus driver signaled that he was about to leave.

"Willard, it looks like the bus is going to pull out. You'd better get on or it'll leave without you."

Willard nodded, picked up his bag and moved toward the bus. Just as he was about to step into the bus, he turned back to Jeff and Reena.

"Jeff, are you sure you really want to stay here? Don't you want to come back with me?"

"Willard, you know as well as I do that I can never go back. This is where I belong now, and I'm content to stay here with Reena. Goodbye, Willard."

"Goodbye, Jeff, and good luck."

With that, Willard turned and stepped into the bus. Inside, he took a seat near the window so he could look out at Jeff and his companion. The bus driver pulled the door closed and started the motor. The motor cranked over and a cloud of black sooty smoke belched out of the tail pipe.

Willard sat there looking through the dusty window at Jeff and his beautiful female companion, Reena. He managed a slight smile, offered up a timid wave and the two waved back. The driver put the motor in gear and released the brake. As the bus pulled away, Willard pressed his face to the window for one final look at Jeff and Reena. Then bus moved through the village and onto the old highway. Willard could no longer see either Jeff or Reena. He knew in his heart that he would never see either of them again.

When Willard returned to New York and went back to the office, he told Damon Cudmore all that had happened in the Yucatan. Cudmore listened attentively without saying a word. When Willard finished telling the entire story, Cudmore simply said, "Well, I'll be damned."

Willard said nothing but sat there and looked back at the big man.

"It's a shame though," continued Cudmore. "I've lost my best copywriter, but maybe it's better this way. Maybe he'll find a form of happiness and contentment that he would never get here."

Willard looked back at the big man in disbelief. Never in all the years that he'd worked at the Cudmore Agency did he see Damon Cudmore exhibit the slightest concern for another human being, and Willard wondered to himself if it was possible for Cudmore, the personification of reptilian indifference, to have a soul? Was it remotely possible that deep within his thick, pachydermal hide there was a small, vestigial trace of human compassion? As he continued to stare at Damon Cudmore, Willard understood that he would never have the answer to those questions; they were to remain life's imponderables.

All Willard could say in a quiet voice was, "Yes sir, it seems that way."

"I'm also stuck with that damn cage down in the sub-basement. Now what am I going to do with that thing?"

"I'm sure you'll think of something, sir," said Willard dryly. "After all, thinking is what you're good at."

"Damn right!" said Cudmore with a broad smile. "Yeah, I'll think of something; I always do."

Willard nodded, then he rose, walked out of Cudmore's office, and went back to the mail room.

Later in the day, he called Dixie Durante to tell her that Jeff was lost in the jungles of the Yucatan and would, most likely, never return to New York. He didn't describe what had happened to Jeff and he did say something about the yellow brick road and the land of Oz. Something in Dixie's tone told Willard that she didn't know what he was talking about and Willard didn't feel like trying to explain.

Anyway, upon hearing that Jeff was lost forever, Dixie immediately started to sob and moan, but to Willard's ear these wailings sounded rather theatrical and lacking in sincerity. After a few minutes of melodramatic mourning, she abruptly calmed down and asked a number of questions about who would be handling Jeff's ad campaigns and who would do the casting for upcoming commercials. Willard began to suspect that she was less concerned about Jeff's disappearance and more concerned about how her career would be affected without him around to give her the small breaks that she needed.

Willard said he didn't know that information, but he was sure that whoever took over for Jeff would surely call her when the right part came around. She seemed consoled by the news. On that note, Willard said goodbye, hung up, and went back to his work.

He had no more contact with the aspiring, bubble-brained actress after that, but later he read in the papers that she'd met and married a tycoon in the real-estate business. Willard also heard that when she married, Dixie had given up her "illustrious stage and screen career" to play the part of a trophy wife for her new-found sugar daddy. Thus, it appeared that Dixie had finally learned the fine art of keeping her mouth shut and saying nothing at social gatherings. In this way nobody ever suspected that behind her two, big, beautiful, blue eyes lay a vast and limitless vacuum that was incapable of containing a single intelligent thought.

After that, life continued at the Cudmore Agency much the same as before Jeff Foxlove had left, except that there was no werewolf caged up in the sub-basement and there were no more werewolf ads and there were no more late-night raids on other advertising agencies.

As for the cage, Damon Cudmore did think of something. He advertised on eBay, a large cage with steel bars for sale; ideal for pet owners with big pets, parents with unruly children, or couples into bondage and sadomasochistic love practices. That pitch hit a responsive chord and in two weeks Cudmore received twelve inquiries from people wanting to buy the cage. He eventually sold and shipped the cage to some guy out in Los Angeles. That man never did explain what he was going to do with Cudmore's steel pen, and Cudmore never asked. He was just happy to be rid of the damn thing and forget about the whole werewolf incident. He did brag, however, that he made a tidy profit when he sold the cage.

With Jeff gone, the infamous wolf attacks ceased and so all of Madison Avenue, and indeed all of New York City, could now rest easy. The police never did uncover the identity of the elusive wolf-perpetrator so they filed the case under the heading of "unsolved murders" and laid it to rest.

Cudmore was right when he said that he'd lost his best copywriter, because Jeff never returned to Madison Avenue. Later, and much to the little mouse-man's surprise, Damon Cudmore promoted Willard to the position of copywriter. Cudmore trained Willard in the trashy art of schlock mongering and in a short time, he was churning out repulsive ads in the raunchy Cudmore style.

Now Willard was never as clever or imaginative as Jeff Foxlove when it came to writing copy that aimed for the jugular, grabbed the consumers by the balls, or seized them by the scruff of the neck but he was nevertheless able to crank out ads that sold the product even if they didn't make sales figures go through the roof. So, Willard continued working as a copywriter in the Cudmore Agency because it was the only job he knew how to do.

One night, a little over a year after his Yucatan trip, Willard found himself working late at the Cudmore Advertising Agency. He was trying hard to write an ad for Twinkle Nest, a feminine douche, and he was wrestling with the concept. He didn't know anything about feminine hygiene products or how women use them, so he didn't have an inkling of what to write, and on this particular night he was struggling with his thoughts. The words just didn't seem to come out right and he couldn't get a handle on putting together a concept that would deliver any sort of message.

After sitting for over an hour before the computer, staring at the blank screen without typing a single word, Willard got up from his desk and walked over to the window. He stood there before the glass and looked out at the cityscape beyond. It was night, most of the tall office buildings were lit up, and they looked like sparkling jewels in the dark of the night. As Willard looked out above the buildings, he saw that the full moon was rising in the sky. It was a big, vivid, beautiful, full orb. Willard watched as the brilliant pearl rose majestically high into the dark, nighttime sky. As he looked at it, his thoughts drifted back to his time with Jeff in the Yucatan.

He thought about that time—the final time he saw Jefferson Foxlove. He remembered his last view of Jeff standing there beside the antiquated old bus with his beautiful, sensuous female companion. And as he thought back to that moment, Willard wondered to himself what had happened to Jeff. Was Jeff still living in that remote part of the Yucatan with his feral companion, the beautiful Reena? Were they still under the spell of the full moon? And were they still running through the primeval jungle at night, side-by-side, hunting together as two creatures of the night, two kindred spirits, two human-beasts with a shared lust?

Well, if so, thought Willard to himself, then maybe Jefferson Foxlove had at last found a truth and reality that was far more honest and far more real than anything that had ever been fabricated in the glass and steel office towers along Madison Avenue.

The End